THE SPIDER:
THE CITY DESTROYER

MASTER OF MEN!
SPIDER®

THE CITY DESTROYER

By Grant Stockbridge

ALTUS PRESS • 2019

CHAPTER 1
"I AM THE SPIDER!"

A MAN and woman stood rigidly against the wall. The man wore rumpled pajamas; the woman's nightgown was green silk and an inset point of lace dipped between her breasts. The window was up and a cold wind flapped the curtains and the woman's nightgown. She was frightened, while the man was very angry.

"For the last time," he said raspingly. "You've got all the papers."

Three men in overcoats faced them and two held automatics carelessly. The third man was scowling at the woman. Abruptly, his head jerked up. He whispered words out the corner of his mouth.

"Quick, Jiggs, the kitchen! Somebody in there!"

The man on his right whirled on his toes, took two quick strides and slapped a swing door open. It banged back against the wood and quivered. Jiggs held it there with his left hand while the muzzle of his gun swept around the kitchen. He grunted, switched on a ceiling light and looked again carefully. He crossed to the kitchen window and found it locked. Jiggs turned off the light once more and went back into the other room. "Nobody in there," he reported. "Must 'a' been the wind."

As he left the kitchen, the narrow door of the broom-closet opened and a hunched figure in a long black cape stepped out.

The entire building was disintegrating, breaking in many places as it fell toward the earth!

Piercing blue gray eyes were narrowed beneath the broad black brim of a slouch hat. There was a thin, mirthless smile on the hunch-back's lips. Without a sound, he glided toward the swing door. His arms crossed; smoothly his hands slid under the cape and two black automatics snouted from his fists. His movements had not seemed hurried, yet the draw was incredibly fast. He stepped into the doorway. "Stand still, you three gentlemen," he said softly, "Keep your hands down."

The three gangsters stiffened their heads snapping up with surprise. The leader twisted his face about, and sudden pallor made his black eyes seem blank holes in his face.

"My God!" he gasped hoarsely. "It's—the Spider!"

The smile still lingered about the mouth of the cloaked man standing in the doorway. "Quite right," he spoke easily. "Deputy Collins—" The tall man in pajamas jerked with surprise at the cripple's knowledge of his name. "Better close that window, and get a blanket for Mrs. Collins. It's quite chilly in here and these rats from New York have no consideration for women even out here."

The Spider's tone was light, but his piercing eyes were intent, and the automatics were like poised cobra heads. He knew the men with whom he had to deal, knew this gang leader, Devil Hackerson, and the deadly gun of Jiggs, the straw-haired hood on his right. He had not expected to find them here tonight when he had wriggled in through the kitchen window, but he was glad now that he had. It would be easier to get the information he must have from this woman and man if the Spider proved his friendliness by helping them out of a jam.

4

He must find out from the woman, especially, what her chemist husband had been working on just before his death a week ago. Police had called the death suicide. The widow—this girl—had insisted it was murder. And her husband's brother, Deputy Sheriff Anse Collins—from Culpeper, Virginia—had come north to investigate. But that death itself was not the important thing....

Two days after the chemist had died, a rich suburban bank in a town fifty miles away had been robbed. The crooks had done something to the steel bars that protected the windows, and the bars had broken like candy sticks. They had done the same thing to the vault and its doors had powdered like cake sugar, beneath the blow of a light sledge hammer. Such a weapon in the hands of unscrupulous criminals could strip the nation's banks.

Obviously some new chemistry of steel had been discovered and had fallen into criminal hands. And Jim Collins, who had died—or been murdered—had been a steel chemist.

These two facts had been associated in the Spider's quick mind and he had once more quit his life of wealth and luxury as Richard Wentworth, scion of riches and of the aristocracy of America for the grim, taut life of the Spider. He had acted quickly, then, following the trail his keen mind had picked for him and he had been barely in time.

SPEEDING NORTHWARD to Middleton where Jim Collins had lived, Wentworth had donned the disguise of the Spider while his faithful Hindu servant, Ram Singh, drove his powerful sedan. He had reached this apartment just in time to find gangsters on the scene, to hear talk of missing papers.

It sounded very much to the Spider as if he had guessed right about Jim Collins and this potent steel destroyer.

Deputy Anse Collins had shut the window and was now picking up a blanket from the davenport where it was obvious he had been sleeping. The girl snuggled it about her body and sat down and tucked her feet up into its warmth. Her blue eyes were harassed and shadows made black smudges beneath them. Honey-colored hair sprawled in delectable disarray about her small, pert head.

"Now, disarm these men," Wentworth told Collins.

The gang leader, Devil Hackerson, still had his head strained around on his shoulder, watching Wentworth. His face was lean and dark, ending in a pointed chin beneath a sneering mouth. There was a Mephistophelian flare to his eyebrows, slanting upward at their outer corners, which, together with his reputation for cold ferocity, had earned him the nickname of "Devil." The man in pajamas was tall, over six feet. He wrenched one gangster's gun away and the man cursed with pain. Collins strode toward Jiggs on Hackerson's right. He moved with angry vehemence, and that very violence tricked him. His foot slipped on the smoothly-waxed floor just as he reached for Jigg's gun. The two men went down together.

"Stand still!" The Spider barked at the other two.

The two men on the floor rolled over and Collins was on top, grappling with the blond gunman. Then suddenly he went limp, soggily, and the snout of Jiggs' gun thrust into view, pointing toward the Spider. But Wentworth had already moved. An agile leap put him at Hackerson's back. The third gangster sprang after him, slashing with a blackjack. The Spider's left gun belched and the man gasped a scream, doubling forward as the bullet took him in the belly. But his flailing arm holding the lead-loaded club swiped at Wentworth, caught him a glancing blow on the side of the head and sent him reeling.

Hackerson saw his chance and whirled with his fist smashing upward.

Wentworth slapped out with his automatic. He didn't want to kill Hackerson because the man knew things that would be invaluable to the Spider. His gun barrel skimmed across Hackerson's forehead, drew a curse of pain and sent the boss gangster reeling backward. Wentworth danced after him, ready to smack him to the floor—and caught swift movement in the corner of his eye. Jiggs was up, springing into the clear to shoot.

The Spider spun on the balls of his feet, threw lead at exactly the same instant. Jiggs caught the slug in the chest and his shoulders slammed back against the wall. He rolled and his clawed hands scraped along the plaster as he went down suddenly on his knees. Wentworth sprang backward toward the kitchen door, guns swiveling. The girl screamed.

Even as she shrieked, Wentworth flung himself face down, headlong on the floor. A bullet thwacked the wall behind him viciously. As he rolled, guessing the cause of his danger, another slug bored the floor beside him.

Now he could see the source of this new menace. The girl was on her feet, her blanket spilled to the floor. Devil Hackerson's thick arm was circled about her from behind, pinning her arms to her side, holding her rigidly in front of him—a motionless unwilling shield. It was a time-worn trick, but it never lost its effectiveness.

Wentworth saw a snub-nosed automatic snouting from behind the girl as he reversed his roll. Lead splintered into the floor again. He jerked up his guns and blasted out the ceiling light. Two guns boomed together, cross-raking the spot where he had lain a moment before. One shot had come from the spot where Jiggs had fallen, on the right, and Wentworth tossed two bullets at the flash. He heard a gun clatter to the floor, heard a man groan in pain. He smiled tightly in the darkness. It sounded as if, this time, Jiggs were out of the battle for good.

The girl screamed again frantically, and the cry was chopped short, muffled by a smacking palm. Two long strides took Wentworth to the sound. He dropped his left gun. Soft warm flesh dented beneath his fingers. His hand slipped upward, gripped a bare shoulder and then he jerked hard. The woman cried out again, seemed to resist, then came toward him with a rush.

WENTWORTH AND the girl reeled backward together. His heels caught in a rug and he tripped, sprawling backward. The girl let out a sobbing gasp of fear and landed heavily on top of him, slamming his head hard against the floor. Warm flesh crushed down on his face, smothering him. It buried an oath in his throat. He rolled from beneath the weeping silken burden, reeled to his feet. His head rang from the nasty crack on the floor but he still clung to his gun. He fought down the drumming in his ears, listened intently. From his right came the bubbling wheezy breath of a man dying with a bullet in his lungs. He knew that would be Jiggs. The woman gasped sobs on the floor. There were only those two sounds....

Wentworth snatched out a pocket flash, sent its small white disc sweeping over the room. Hackerson was gone. The Spider pivoted on his heel, sped into the kitchen and flung up the window. He whistled eerily, a three-noted bar, and an instantaneous reply came from below. With a grunt of satisfaction, he darted back to the scene of the hasty battle. That whistle had ordered his faithful Hindu servant, Ram Singh, to take the trail. He would spot the fugitive and pursue him relentlessly.

The kitchen light flung an oblong of luminousness out into the living room, just reaching Collins, who was still unconscious. Wentworth stooped over the deputy sheriff, found a welted red knot behind his left ear where Jigg's gun had struck. A slosh of water from the kitchen and the man stirred, moaning. Wentworth watched him a moment, then nodded and stopped fleetingly by each of the two men he had slain. He pressed something that glinted to each forehead and when he stepped away, a blob that was red as their spilled blood glowed upon the brow of each. That blob had sprawling hairy legs, and viciously ready fangs— *the seal of the Spider!*

A thin mocking grin was on the Spider's lips as he left his prey, reloaded and holstered his guns, and crossed to the woman. She lay face down on the floor, arms thrown protectingly over her blond head. Her silken gown hung from her in tatters, exposing the smooth tense curve of her back.

Wentworth dropped the blanket over her. "The gangsters are gone," he said swiftly, "but police will be here within minutes and I must be gone when they arrive. You know by now that the Spider is your friend. You must answer some questions."

The girl stirred slightly, and he helped her sit up on the floor. Her eyes were red-rimmed. She locked her even white teeth upon her lower lip and fought down sobs. Wentworth drew the blanket about her shoulders and squatted before her.

"I'll tell you what I know," Wentworth said swiftly, and recounted what he had learned of her husband's death.

While he spoke, the girl's eyes quested over the room. She saw the dead men and her eyes flew back to Wentworth as if for protection. Her gaze clung desperately to him now.

"I want to know what invention your husband was working on," Wentworth said. "Can you tell me?"

The girl shook her golden head. Her hair slipped down across her shoulder. "Those gangsters were after something like that, too," she said. "They wanted something they said was in Jim's papers. But it wasn't there."

"You don't know what it was?"

"No, except Jim said—" she choked and her eyes filled. "Jim said it would put us on Easy Street forever. We could…could…" Her voice died out.

Wentworth heard Collins stir behind him and jerked his head about. The deputy surged abruptly to his feet, stood with clenched fists, his eyes darting about. He took in the twisted bodies on the floor, glared at Wentworth. "One of them got away," he growled hoarsely.

"Do you know what Jim's invention was?" Wentworth asked sharply.

The man's dark eyes narrowed. "I reckon it wouldn't be any of your business if I did," he said.

WENTWORTH STRAIGHTENED. "That's where you're wrong," he said coldly. "Two days after Jim Collins died," a  rich bank was robbed near Middletown here. The crooks who broke into that bank had something brand new in the way of burglar tools. It smashed steel like sugar. I associate your brother's death with that robbery."

Deputy Collins came forward slowly. He was a heavily built man, over six feet tall, with wedge shoulders. His neck was corded. "I reckon you'll have to explain that last remark," he said. His voice was soft and slow, but there was a hard ring to the words.

Wentworth uttered an impatient exclamation. He knew the police must be close. He could not understand why they had not come before this.

"I mean that gangsters murdered your brother for his secret," he said swiftly. "Now, for heaven's sake, if you know anything, spill it fast."

The huge man stared at him with his big head thrust forward, the heavy shock of brown hair tousled. He seemed to be studying the man beneath the false face that Wentworth had built over his own to create the character of the Spider.

"I reckon we do owe you a mite of consideration," Collins said slowly. "You sure pulled us out of a powerful tight hole."

He shook his head. "We don't know much. Only that Jim was figuring on selling his invention to the government. But there's two men that know more than we do. They're Bill Butterworth, who worked with Jim at the steel plant, and…" A scowl twisted the man's features. "DeHaven Alrecht, a damned foreigner who had his finger in Jim's pie."

Nancy Collin's quiet voice broke in. "Mr. Alrecht was very nice to us, Anse," she said. "He got Jim his job at the plant and he was going to finance the invention when Jim got it finished."

"Sure, for a lion's-share cut of the profits," Anse Collins drawled. "And you can't tell me he was just being nice to Jim. I always did think the skunk had his eye on you."

"Anse!" The girl's voice was distressed.

"It's a fact," Anse Collins said stubbornly. "Alrecht was dead set on marrying you."

A thunderous fist beat on the door. Wentworth sprang to his feet "That's the police," he snapped. "Listen, the crooks who held you up came from New York. If you want to find Jim's murderers, you can go there and register at the Kennillworth Hotel on Forty-Sixth Street. I'll get in touch with you."

He reached the kitchen door in a bound—checked short. Crouched on the fire-escape was a policeman. The cold light from the window glinted on his badge and on a gun in his hand. So that was why the police had delayed! They had surrounded the building before knocking. The fist battered at the door again.

"Open up," a man shouted. "It's the police."

The fire-escape and door were blocked. That policeman on the fire-escape prevented any use of the dumb-waiter in the

12

kitchen. And here on the floor lay the bodies of two men with the seal of the Spider upon their foreheads. What did it matter that they were criminals? The Spider had killed them, and the law could not consider motives.

"If you don't open up in one minute," the rough voice bellowed from the hall, "we'll break the door in!"

CHAPTER 2
RAM SINGH FALLS

THE TWO, Nancy Collins, and her brother-in-law, were staring at Wentworth with worried frowns. Unconsciously, the girl drew the blanket more tightly about her. There was a wary light in Anse Collins' eyes.

"Look here," he shouted gruffly. "I'm an officer of the law, too, even if I haven't any authority here. Reckon you better get out of here damned quick."

Wentworth laughed softly. "That's right. Stall them as long as you can."

He darted into the bed room, slapped the door shut and locked it. He heard the reverberations of more pounding on the outside door, heard Collins' gruff voice, but couldn't make out the words. He reached the window with quick strides. It was already raised and he peered furtively toward the man on the fire-escape. The cop was still poised there with gun in hand, peering into the kitchen.

A glance above and below showed still another uniform cap thrust over the edge of the roof, two shadows that were men in

13

the alley below. Wentworth's smile became grim. It was almost as if these men knew that the Spider was here and were taking no chances on his escape. There was a fifty-thousand-dollar reason for him—the rewards piled upon his head by communities he had flouted and mocked in his swift and deadly pursuit of evildoers.

It did not matter at all that Wentworth had done these things only in the name of justice, that he killed only when justice was served by death. A dozen different states were ready to hang or electrocute him—if they could once identify him as the Spider. And in the other room there was evidence enough of that, besides the two persons who knew he had affixed the mocking crimson seal to the dead men lying there.

If he failed to escape, not only was his life forfeit, but perhaps with him would die the chance of capturing criminals who, through their wide scientific knowledge, could ravage from banks all over the nation the hard-earned savings of thousands of honest men and women. Even as he thought this, he wheeled, reentered the living-room. There was one slim chance of escape, but he would have to act quickly.

Collins and Nancy jerked about as he opened the door. "Stand clear," he ordered them gesturing toward the portal where police hammered.

Collins sprang back and Wentworth fired twice into the ceiling. A fusillade answered, riddling the door. Wentworth sprang back into the bedroom, reached the window in a bound.

The cop on the fire-escape straightened, smashed in the window with his gun, sprang inside. But that man on the roof and those two in the alley still watched. Wentworth shrugged. It was now or never. Already the police were at the door of the bedroom.

"Open up, Spider," a man commanded. "We got you dead to rights this time. You're surrounded and you can't get away."

There was jubilance in the voice, eager triumph. Wentworth's smile tightened. He whipped a length of silken cord from beneath his arm, cord that was not quite so large in diameter as a pencil, yet which had a tensile strength of seven-hundred pounds. He looped it over the steam radiator beneath the window, forked the sill and slid down the side of the building with the cord wrapped about arms and legs. He contrived to make a lot of noise doing it, kicked the window out of the room below the Collins' bedroom.

The two policemen on watch in the alley heard and shouted rapidly. They ran down the alley with their flashlights questing over the side of the building.

"Don't shoot!" Wentworth cried in terror-stricken accents. "For God's sake, don't shoot!"

He pushed his feet against the side of the house and caused himself to swing from side to side. The cops ran down the alley until they stood below him but carefully away from the wall so that he could not drop upon them. Wentworth had descended another story now. He was only two floors above the ground and directly opposite the window of another apartment.

Windows were flung open above his head and becapped heads thrust out. "We got him," the cops below sang out triumphantly.

Wentworth was gyrating widely on his silken line now. His feet struck the window and crashed it inward. Then, abruptly, the Spider vanished. He swung into the window and out of sight. Guns blazed in the alley. Men shouted excitedly.

Inside the room where Wentworth crouched, a quavering voice said, "Don't shoot me. I ain't got nothing you want."

Wentworth crossed to the door in a bound, sprang across the room beyond and jerked open the outside door, slammed it again. Silently then, he slipped back to the kitchen. This apartment had exactly the same floor plan as the Collins' rooms and he had no trouble in finding his way. In the kitchen, he went directly to the dumb-waiter shaft. The cage itself was one story below and he hauled it quietly to his level and climbed inside. He was certain the basement would be guarded. There was still only a slim chance of escaping. He raised the dumbwaiter slowly until he was once more level with the Collins apartment. He

RICHARD WENTWORTH

listened intently, ear to the shaft door. There was no sound in the apartment and he eased into the empty kitchen.

Then he could hear talking in the next room, Nancy Collins

protesting vigorously that she knew nothing except what she had told. Wentworth peered into the room. Collins was standing with legs aggressively braced, his tousled head thrust forward. "I reckon you-all have asked enough questions now," the big man drawled quietly.

THERE WERE two police inside, one in civilian clothes, one in uniform. Wentworth's spring into the room was soundless. The first warning the two men had of his presence was the flashing light within their skulls when his pistols slapped their heads. Collins half-started forward, but suddenly he was looking into the black muzzle of an automatic.

"I don't want to slap you down, too," the Spider said softly.

Anse Collins grinned slowly. "Reckon I don't want you to either," he smiled.

Wentworth nodded. He stooped and snatched the uniformed man's cap, put it on and whirled back to the kitchen, clambered out on the fire-escape. The two police were still in the alley.

"He went down the dumb-waiter!" Wentworth yelled at them. "The Spider's in the basement!"

The two cops peered up and saw the silhouette of a police cap against the sky.

"Get down in the basement, you lugs!" Wentworth bawled. "He's down there, I tell you. I'll watch the alley."

The two cops hesitated a moment longer, then raced for the cellar entrance as Wentworth clattered down. They paused once more at the door. Wentworth dropped from the fire-escape and ran toward them. They ducked out of sight. He clapped the door shut behind them, jammed into its crack a thin piece of rasp steel from the tool kit beneath his arm. Then he raced on for the street. The cops in the basement started shouting. Their guns banged, smashing the door's lock. The man on the roof peered down uncertainly into the darkness of the alley, but it sounded to him as if Spider and police had joined battle in the basement.

Wentworth darted into the street, saw a line of police cars at the curb and leaped into the first. The motor was still hot and it started instantly. He took the corner on two whistling tires. Behind him, through the whine and sough of the wind roaring past the car, biting at his silk-gloved hands, he heard the popping of pistol shots, the skirl of whistles, then the wail of sirens. But he had a two-block lead. It was all the Spider needed.

Ten minutes later, driving his own car and stripped of the disguise of the Spider which was carefully hidden in a secret compartment in the car's rear, Richard Wentworth parked by the Ft. Middle Hotel, where he had registered that night with Ram Singh. He had several lines of investigation open, but just now it was most important that he be here to receive a phone call from Ram Singh when the Hindu should have located the headquarters toward which Devil Hackerson had been fleeing. He had hardly reached his room when the bell tinkled and he snatched up the receiver.

"*Sahib!*" It was Ram Singh's voice, a gasp of haste.

"Shoot," Wentworth ordered.

"The Sky Building, *"sahib,"* Ram Singh blurted. "They are pl—"

The sound of a shot and a groan echoed faintly over the wire. Wentworth's hands tensed about the phone, knuckles whitening.

"Ram Singh!" he called anxiously.

There was a soft click of disconnection. Frantically, Wentworth signaled the operator. "That call, where did it come from?"

"From New York City, sir," the telephone operator reported.

Wentworth waited five dragging minutes while she raised the New York operator, while she reported that the call came from a telephone pay-station in a Bronx drug store.

"Notify police that there was a shooting at that address," Wentworth snapped. "I heard it over the telephone."

He slammed up the receiver and flung from the hotel, sprang behind the wheel of his car and sent it sizzling along the one hundred and forty mile stretch to New York. He did not think the police would reach the spot in time to learn anything. His mouth shut with compressed lips that formed a straight bitter line. The underworld always struck at the Spider through his loved ones: through Nita van Sloan, the woman he loved, through his loyal Hindu. If Ram Singh had been killed, Wentworth would rip New York's underworld to pieces to find his murderer!

Meanwhile, what of Ram Singh's message? It was clear that some deviltry was afoot at the Sky Building. Were the users of the steel crusher planning a robbery there?

WHILE WENTWORTH raced for New York, while police radio prowl cars sped to the spot where Ram Singh had been shot, Ram Singh himself lay unconscious on the floor of a gray sedan beneath the feet of two men. One of those was Devil Hackerson, and the frown between his eyes was increasing the satanic slant of his brows. "This is damned foolishness," he snapped. "I'm going to stick a knife into the nigger's guts and dump him in the gutter."

The other man turned his head very slowly. "If you do, the Master will cut off your supply of the stuff," he said. His voice was high; he whined slightly, but there was a tone of insolent authority.

Hackerson cursed violently. The driver echoed his anger. "This here guy we shot works for the Spider," the latter said. "We ought to string him up by his ears."

The third man said nothing more. He sat and stared straight ahead through the windshield at the Fifth Avenue traffic through which they were weaving a slow and laborious way. He had a high dome of a head that seemed to swell out behind the ears and dwarf the little, wizened face. One of his overly prominent eyes had a cast in it and was a pale, washed-out blue. The other was brown and kept darting about like a frightened bird. He lipped a cigarette wetly.

"Listen, Devil," he whined. "You know I ain't got nothing to do with this. All I do is get the orders over the telephone and bring 'em to you. This guy what calls himself the Master always seems to know where to find me. He may call me at a restaurant or in a saloon and sometimes at the boarding-house. I don't see no harm in doing what the Master says. We get good dough out of it and if you don't do what he says, I'll lose my job, and…."

Devil Hackerson pushed the other roughly in the face, but without ill nature, and the man's cap slid off. He was bald as an egg.

"Don't get excited, Baldy," he said. "We're doing what your

Master wants." There was a sneer in his voice at the word "Master."

"But it's not to save your job. It's because we want the stuff. Boy, with that, we could knock over the Treasury of the United States without any trouble, at all."

The man called Baldy drew the cap over his bald head with nervous hands. "The Master says next time you don't use the stuff for what he tells you, you don't get any more." Baldy's voice was trembling, a little squeaky with fear at the message, but he kept on with it. "He says tell you there are other guys would be glad to get their hands oh the stuff."

"Ain't it the truth?" murmured Hackerson, but the frown on his forehead was puzzled now. "I'll be damned if I can see what good it'll do to knock the Sky Building down in the streets. Still more, I can't see why we got to take this nigger up on top of it and wait until the building topples before he dies. Hell, she might fall over while we're up there since it's all fixed now."

Ram Singh heard the words with a sense of dull shock. These men talked of making the world's tallest building collapse as if it were no more than a hill of sand on the beach. Yet the Sky Building's collapse, even in the dead of night, would kill hundreds. And by day with the thousands teeming past on Fifth Avenue… Ram Singh shuddered involuntarily, listened while Baldy talked on.

"There's not enough wind," Baldy said. "The stone walls will hold it together until we have a good wind, and then…" He paused. Mere words couldn't paint for him the collapse of that mighty building, its base covering an entire city block, its tower more than a fifth of a mile above the streets. There was a gleam in his brown eye and his tongue slid out like a timid pink snake to touch his dry lips. "The Weather Bureau says the wind will keep rising until it reaches gale force about morning."

Ram Singh groaned and stirred beneath their feet Hackerson leaned forward, grinding the muzzle of his gun into Ram Singh's neck.

"Keep quiet, black-boy," he rasped, "or I'll crack you again."

There was a drying red stain on Ram Singh's left shoulder.

"Hadn't we better get him up on the seat now, put his robe around him?" Baldy asked timidly.

DEVIL HACKERSON jerked erect, thrust his satanic face into Baldy's cowering countenance. "Listen," he rasped, "you can bring orders from this guy that calls himself the Master, but you're not running my mob, see?" Baldy cringed back into his corner and made placating sounds with his mouth. Hackerson chuckled. He caught Ram Singh by his wounded shoulder and yanked him to a sitting position, threw a black robe around him and hauled him up on the seat.

"You're the Yogi Mala Kalai Balu," said Hackerson, "and you're just finishing a long fast. Furthermore, you've made a pledge not to speak again in this life. If you show any inclination to forget that, I'm going to remind you with lead in your guts. Get it?"

Ram Singh was weak with his wound. His face had a gray tinge beneath its swarthy skin. "I understand," he replied slowly.

When the sedan stopped before the Sky Building, Hackerson helped the Hindu to alight with every show of deference and the car rolled away. Baldy peering back with his one good eye from the rear seat. Ram Singh could hardly stand. He leaned heavily on his captor's arm and together they went upward to the tower. There were few persons about to stare curiously at the two. Within a half hour, the tower would close. Ram Singh's eyes were on the floor. His head seemed too heavy to lift.

In his dull thoughts, he sought frantically for some way to escape. But there was none that did not involve ridding himself of this gangster at his side, and unarmed, he had not the strength for the attempt. He had managed to get two words out to the Spider before that bullet had crashed him to the floor of the booth—before gunmen had charged into the store and taken him out while they held clerks and customers of the drug store at pistol point. God grant that those two words had been enough!

It seemed incredible to Ram Singh that these gangsters, because of orders received through that queer spokesman, were wrecking this huge building. But the "stuff," as they called it, already had been loosed upon the mighty girders. The supports were undermined, ready to crumple into powdery fragments whenever the wind blew hard. And thousands would be crushed to pulp beneath it.

"Hurry up," snapped Hackerson. "I don't like the way the wind is moaning."

He waited his chance and—shoved Ram Singh into a porter's closet where brushes and pails were stored for use at night. No one would enter it until late the next night when the cleaning got under way again and before then....

"Heavy wind blowing up," Hackerson gibed at Ram Singh. "You won't have long to wait, I guess."

He gagged the Hindu brutally, bound him hand and foot, lashed him to the pipes of a slop sink in the closet. Then he kicked him in the stomach. "Baldy said to knock you out," he jeered, "but I'd rather you could hear the wind rising and feel the building sway just before she topples. You ought to enjoy that."

He kicked Ram Singh again, shut the door and locked it. Ram Singh did not hear him go, but he heard something else. He heard the hollow moan of wind in the elevator shafts and the hallways. He had felt tall skyscrapers sway before this, when they were held together by the flexibility of the steel that had enabled man to rear buildings higher and higher into the skies.

But now the steel was no longer flexible. Now it would crumble and split when the strain was put upon it. Was it his imagination tricking him or was stately rhythmic movement of the building a little jerky? By Kali and by Siva, the doom of the Sky Building, of the thousands its fall would kill, was already upon it.

Ram Singh strained against his ropes. It wrenched his wounded shoulder and he groaned feebly against his gag. Blackness swarmed about him. Through it he could feel the sickening sway of the building, hear the mounting wail of the wind as if it already mourned the dead....

CHAPTER 3
WHEN THOUSANDS DIED

WENTWORTH HAD a blowout on the way to New York City. The eastern sky was graying when he skidded to a halt before the Centre Street headquarters of the New York City police and took the steps three at a time. It was just after seven o'clock—but the winter dawn came late—and there was a chance that Stanley Kirkpatrick, the commissioner, might be at his desk.

The sergeant in the anteroom recognized Wentworth, nodded alertly. "Commissioner's in his office, sir," he said. "Shall I…?

He stared at a vanishing back as Wentworth pushed into the private office of the police commissioner. Kirkpatrick's head came up sharply at the abrupt entrance; his eyes narrowed as they saw the tightness of Wentworth's face.

"What is it, Dick?" he asked quickly.

"Ram Singh!" Wentworth snapped out. "That shooting scrape on Jerome Avenue!"

Kirkpatrick stared, frowning, thumbed through a file of reports on his desk, paused to study one. "Unidentified man, apparently a Negro, shot in a telephone-booth and carried off by assailants," he summarized swiftly.

Wentworth cursed harshly, dropped into a chair and sat stiffly on six inches of the seat. His fists were clenched on his knees.

"They got Ram Singh," he said dully.

The two men, Wentworth and Kirkpatrick, were much alike in a general way as they sat there facing each other—two men who had been—violent enemies and now were friends. Both were dark and had lean, hard jaws. Kirkpatrick had a saturnine countenance, harsh lines chiseled about a firm-lipped mouth that was emphasized by a straight pointed mustache. His gray eyes peered out straightly from under broad, level brows and his black hair lay flat against his head. There was a calmness about the man as he rested his elbows on the desk and rubbed his palms together with a dry whisper of sound. "Tell me about it," he urged, his voice incisive, accents clipped.

Wentworth nodded. "You know what the Spider did in Middleton tonight?" he queried, and when Kirkpatrick nodded, Wentworth explained that he had set Ram Singh to searching for Devil Hackerson since one of the men killed by the Spider in Middleton was a Hackerson hood.

There was a slight ironic twist of Kirkpatrick's lips as he listened that had nothing to do with the seriousness of the situation. His mockery was because both of them spoke of the Spider as though he were a third person.

Kirkpatrick had battled the Spider for many months, though secretly he admired and respected this swift avenger who struck down the criminals that the law-hedged police could not reach. Finally he had confronted Wentworth, told him flatly that he knew he was the Spider, but that he lacked proof. Until such time as positive evidence fell into his hands, he said, he would assist Wentworth and the Spider in every legal way. But if that evidence came into his possession, he would prosecute to the full extent of his powers. It was an armed truce. Never again had either of them referred to Wentworth's possible connection with

the Spider. But it often amused Kirkpatrick, and the mockery touched Wentworth's face, too.

His gray-blue eyes met Kirkpatrick's directly as he talked, explaining about the Spider's activities in Middleton, how they confirmed his own suspicion that there was a tie-up between the death of the chemist, Jim Collins, and the robbery of the bank. But there was mockery in Wentworth's tip-tilted eyebrows though there was grave seriousness in the set, determined mouth and chin, the thin-bridged intelligent nose, the calm broad forehead. His black hair crisped across his brow, swept down to hide a thin scar upon his right temple, relic of an old knife fight. There was a throbbing in that wound now, but that was the only symptom in his vital, keen face that the alarm over Ram Singh gnawed at his heart.

"You see the seriousness of what threatens," Wentworth said swiftly. "If these criminals use their steel-eater widely, there won't be a bank in the country safe from their attack. Just before Ram Singh was—" Wentworth paused and swallowed hard; the muscles bulged along his jaw line, "before he was shot, he shouted something about the Sky Building. I don't know whether he meant a robbery was being staged there or whether he meant Hackerson had a headquarters there. But if you are willing, I'd like to go there with you and see what we can discover."

KIRKPATRICK NODDED gravely, but it was nearly two hours later—two hours in which they had thrown every resource of the police into the search for Ram Singh—that Kirkpatrick stepped to a wardrobe in a corner and shrugged into a dark-blue belted topcoat. He set a derby straight across his brows and together he and Wentworth strode from the building.

The commissioner's heavy private car made swift speed through the thickening traffic. The wind whipped past the closed windows with a thin whining, and though there was a heater in the tonneau, their breath made small wavering puffs before their mouths as they talked.

"If they bothered to carry Ram Singh away," Kirkpatrick mused. "It's likely he was only wounded."

"Probably," Wentworth agreed. He stared out at the stone buildings, gray in the early morning light as they slid past. The car had swept up Lafayette now, spun west to Fifth Avenue and was stepping north along the broad thoroughfare. Men and women struggled against the wind as against a savage undertow, coats whipping about their thighs.

"The tail end of that Hatteras gale is hitting here today," Kirkpatrick said absently. "The Sky Building will be rocking like a tree." Wentworth nodded again, wordlessly. He was trying to think what Ram Singh could have meant by that last shout about the Sky Building. "They are pl..." he had got out just before the shot. Perhaps that last word had been "planning," but planning what? Wentworth could not guess at Ram Singh's fearful secret, at the horror that tortured the faithful Hindu now, wounded and a prisoner of tight ropes, as he struggled for freedom high in the groaning Sky Building.

How could Wentworth guess that the Sky Building was slated for destruction, that even now its weakened steel girders were yielding beneath the lash of the rising wind? He knew, of

31

course, of the steel-eater, but why would anyone wish to raze the building? Even Devil Hackerson, who had carried out the orders for the Master and put the "stuff" on the girders, had not been able to understand why it should be destroyed.

As they sped farther north, the sidewalks were thick with crowds of people going to work. It was a little after nine, the height of the rush hour. Girls ducked their heads into the wind, pulled their coats tight about their hips and plunged across the street on their high heels. Men ploughed doggedly into the rising gale's thrust clasping hats to their heads with freezing hands. Even from the car, the cherry red of cold-burnt ears could be seen, but Wentworth beheld the tapestry of New York going to work only subconsciously. His mind was still busy with the problem of Rani Singh and the Sky building.

The squat broad base of the building came into sight, hinting even in the briefly truncated view below the auto roof of the majesty that soared above. Wentworth, alighting from the car, paused on the sidewalk, holding his derby firmly in place while he leaned back to peer up at the heights that rose a fifth of a mile into the sky. Sunlight glinted coldly on the strips of chromium that streaked its sides, but bustling gray clouds would soon blot that out. The gale was on the way. It would soon be blowing sixty miles an hour and better up there where the rounded dome of the dirigible mooring-mast met the clouds.

Wentworth frowned, walked into the elaborate lobby with Kirkpatrick at his side. Kirkpatrick looked sideways at him curiously. It was rarely that his friend was so preoccupied, engrossed though he might be in the battles of mankind, in the defense of humanity against the underworld.

"Just what do we do now that we're here?" he asked.

"I'm not quite sure," Wentworth confessed.

HE ASKED some apparently aimless questions of the elevator starter and learned that nothing out of the ordinary had occurred in the building. He knew already that there had been no robbery reports from the vicinity the night before. He turned away abruptly, stalked to Kirkpatrick's side. He had a feeling that the answer to his bewilderment was within reach, but that he could not fathom it. It was within reach all right, no farther away than the thick walls that encased the steel basic supports of the building, eaten by the Master's "stuff" until they would crack when the strain of the gale came....

"Let's go up to the tower," Wentworth said abruptly. "I always get a thrill out of the sway in windy weather, out of the feeling of power in man's conquest of the elements."

Kirkpatrick smiled wryly. "Seeking inspiration, Dick?"

Wentworth nodded shortly. "I have a feeling that the answer is right here." He stretched out his gloved hand and closed the fingers palm upward. "But I can't quite grasp it. Something tells me that I know everything that is essential to finding the answer."

The elevator was wafted upward silently. Through the shaft, the wind moaned and made hollow bass whinings. While they were moving the sway of the building was not noticeable, but once they reached the observation room, it could be felt. Kirkpatrick looked about him with alert, quick glances. There were no visitors to the tower so early in the morning.

"You may like this swaying business, but I don't care for it at all," Kirkpatrick said.

"The building is entirely safe," Wentworth said shortly, staring about also, looking out over the city where the wind was snatching smoke from the chimneys, dancing bits of paper high in the air. "Engineers always allow a safety margin of three or four hundred percent in stresses. They probably did more than that here."

A particularly strenuous gust howled about the corners of the building, and somewhere deep in the building there was a faint, creaking groan.

Kirkpatrick grimaced. "I still don't like it," he muttered. "Are you going up any higher?"

Wentworth looked out once more over the gale-lashed city and nodded slowly. "I think I shall," he said. "There is something about wind…" He paused and cocked his head, listening. Above the screaming of the wind, he caught a faint regular sound, a muffled *thump, thump, thump*.

"Do you hear that?" Wentworth asked quickly.

Kirkpatrick frowned at him. "I hear the wind and I hear the building making funny noises."

Wentworth moved his hand impatiently. "I don't mean that. I mean a sound like someone knocking. Listen."

They listened again to that faint muffled *thump, thump, thump*. On its heels came another sound from deep in the bowels of the building. Another creaking groan.

"Listen, Wentworth," Kirkpatrick's face was worried, "I'll swear this budding is creaking."

Wentworth did not hear him. He was striding rapidly around a corner of the hall whence the thumping seemed to come. He stood there, waiting. Once more the sound reached his ears, more loudly this time. With a subdued cry, he sprang to the door of a porter's closet. He tried the knob, found it locked. His hand flew to the Spider's tool kit beneath his arm and rapidly he forced the lock. Kirkpatrick came around the corner just as the bolt snicked back and Wentworth yanked the door open.

Together they peered into the half-dark. Brooms and mops were stacked against the wall, pails were on the floor and among the pails lay something that moved. Wentworth splashed light from a pocket flash into the gloom and a cry spilled from his lips: "Ram Singh!"

THE HINDU had beaten on the door with his bound feet. Now he tossed and bumped on the floor. He made fearful sounds behind his gag. Wentworth flung down on his knees, yanked away the cloth that blocked Ram Singh's speech.

"Quickly, *sahib!*" the Hindu's voice sounded sepulchral as it croaked from his dry throat. "Quickly! This building is going to fall!"

"What?" It was a startled curse from Kirkpatrick.

"God!" Wentworth barked. "That's it! Those fiends have put the steel-eater on the girders of this building! I knew the answer was here!"

He was hauling Ram Singh from the close confines of the closet, slicing off his bonds with a pocket knife.

35

"That is it, *sahib*," the Hindu gasped. "They left me here to die as a warning to..." He choked off the words, coughed down the "to the Spider," he had started to say. "They say that when the wind blows strong, it will fall."

The three men stood rigid, heard once more the groaning complaint of the building. It seemed louder than before. It seemed the moan of a living, suffering thing. As if all the thousands of men and women in the building knew what was about to happen and had joined their voices in one vast moan of universal terror. For an instant the sound held them in the grip like paralysis. They felt the building sway giddily... Unconsciously, they leaned the opposite way as if by their feeble weight they would counterbalance the catastrophe that loomed. Their hearts thumped swiftly, for they felt that doom was upon them.

"We're gone," said Kirkpatrick flatly. His face was white beneath its lean tan.

The sway ended. The building seemed to poise on the split edge of oblivion, then there was a slight jerk. It wavered back into the wind. Wentworth snapped from his motionlessness.

"We must clear the building, clear the streets and the neighboring places!" he poured out words. "Kirk, you get the reserves! I'll call out the fire department, send an alarm...."

He sprang into the main hall, flung a swift glance about, spotted a red box and sprang to it with an eager cry. He smashed the glass. An elevator operator gaped at him with open mouth.

"Where's the fire?" he demanded.

"This building is going to collapse!" Wentworth snapped. "The steel girders have been cut." He whirled to Ram Singh.

"Get downstairs and tell them to stop everyone at the doors and send them away, let the elevators rise empty and take out people as fast as they can." He thrust a courtesy police badge into Ram Singh's hand for authority.

"Operator, take this man down and don't stop until you hit the first floor!"

Wentworth ran for a phone, heard Kirkpatrick's crisp voice barking orders into a transmitter in a public booth. His words came out swiftly, but clipped and precise as if he sat in his own office directing activities.

Wentworth stared out the window at the evidence of the wind's power, heard the still mounting volume of its shrieks about the building. Now he was oversensitive to each fractional sway of the skyscraper. He smiled grimly to think that within seconds this huge tower of stone and crumbling steel would crash its hundreds of human souls into extinction.

He was bitter with himself for having failed to guess the answer long before, but he could see no way in which he could have figured it out. It was a piece of murderous criminality without parallel. Even now that he knew what impended, he could discern no motive. What possible reason or profit could there be?

He took a cigarette from his platinum case and smiled grimly at his unwavering hands. They wouldn't shake even in hell! But he was shaking inwardly, not in personal fear, but with dread of the horror that impended for the city's millions. He fought himself to calmness. His eyes gazing past the steady flame of his lighter spotted a NO SMOKING sign. The smile twisted on his lips. He blew out smoke and Kirkpatrick slammed out of the booth. He stopped short at sight of Wentworth calmly smoking, drew in a quivering breath. There was grayness beneath the tan of his face, but Wentworth's steadiness braced him. He nodded in approval.

BOTH OF them must keep their heads, even in face of this overwhelming catastrophe, if they were to, snatch the victims from imminent doom. They must forget themselves… The flame wavered as he lighted a cigarette.

"Suppose you and I take alternate floors and empty them," Wentworth suggested. "We'll clear them until reserves can arrive and take over. I sent word to the business office of the building and they're organizing the elevator banks now."

"I'll take the floor below this," Kirkpatrick agreed. "You take the one below that."

Once more the building swayed and groaned. This time there could be no doubt as to the cause of the sound. Wentworth checked his cigarette half way to his mouth, his eyes widening, his mouth feeling dry. Was this the last sway? Was the building heeling over into the final dive to destruction? Slowly the Sky Tower braced back into the push of the wind; the groan faded into a dim creak. Wentworth found he was holding his breath and he blew it out noisily.

"There's about a forty mile wind now," he said, clearing the hoarseness from his throat. "My guess is that when she hits fifty, the building goes."

They stared into each other's eyes and their smiles were forced. They went swiftly down the steps together. At the floor below, they paused for a moment on the platform, facing each other. Their palms touched briefly in a hand-clasp—two lean-faced men with death upon them, but with small smiles on their lips.

"See you in hell," Wentworth said trying to make it sound like a joke. He snapped his cigarette into a corner, clattered down stairs and into an office. People were standing excitedly; the fire gong was dinning, but they all thought it was a false alarm. How could the Sky Building burn?

"Get out quickly!" Wentworth shouted at them. "There's no danger if you move quickly and in orderly fashion. There'll be an elevator here in a moment. Wait in the hall."

"What's the matter?" a man demanded harshly. He was fat-cheeked and fat-bodied, but his clothes fitted faultlessly. "We have business to do and haven't any time for fire drills."

Wentworth eyed him coldly, his mouth grim. "If your business is more important than your life, by all means stay," he barked. "Your workers are leaving. This whole building will go within ten minutes."

Women squealed; a few men laughed. One said something about being nonchalant and tried to light a cigarette, but the flame danced in his trembling fingers and went out. The workers filed swiftly from the office. Wentworth had no trouble in the other offices. He simply held open the door so that those within could see the other people waiting in the hall. While he was in the second office, the first elevator took on a load.

CHAPTER 4
FLIGHT FROM DOOM!

A PERSISTENT worry thrust through the horror in Wentworth's brain. If the building swayed and failed to come back, the elevators would be blocked even if the structure did not topple at once. Hundreds would be trapped, helpless. The stairs would be too slow....

"Women in the elevators," Wentworth barked. "Men, down the steps!"

A man began to curse shrilly. "Walk down ninety stories! You're a damned fool."

Wentworth drew his automatics, a small white smile on his lips.

"Walk down," he ordered, "or I'll let you have it!"

The men walked. Wentworth's mind kept veering to the tragedy at hand. He tried to estimate the chances of escape for those hundreds and his head jerked in a tense negative. The cords of his neck felt stiff and hard. No matter how rapidly they moved, scores would die—millions of dollars worth of buildings would be ground to powder. And all to satisfy the mysterious criminal plans of some monstrous killer.

When the third cage stopped at his floor, a policeman stepped out and saluted. "I'm taking over, sir," he said.

Wentworth nodded tightly. "I've got the men walking down," he said. "The idea is that as soon as the women are out on all floors, well start picking up the men."

"Okay," the policeman said. He turned to the crowd. "Get

a move on there," his hearty voice rang out. "Think you got all day? In about ten minutes this building is going to fall down! And boy, oh boy, it will go boom!"

Wentworth forced a laugh and men and women joined. It was nervous laughter and shrill, but it was better than the white-faced silence and fear. Wentworth stopped to light a cigarette before he strolled to the steps. Still his hand did not shake. The women, huddled together, watched him with wide, frightened eyes. He smiled at them and it took all his courage to make that smile genuine. So many of them—and he, too—might never reach the street alive. He lifted his hat politely… Kirkpatrick, walking also, met him on the steps.

"The police have taken over," he said sharply. "They're clearing the other buildings and the streets are roped off for twelve blocks around. Ram Singh collapsed and was shipped to a hospital."

Wentworth swore. "I'd forgotten his wound. He was too eager to help to mention it. That man deserves a medal if anyone…" He broke off, rigid in his tracks. A shivering groan filled the air about them. A thin white snow of plaster sifted through the air and before their eyes, a crack gaped in the wall of the stairs. A man behind them screamed and bolted downward.

Wentworth pivoted and smacked him down with a right to the jaw.

"Hold it," he ordered sharply, shouting at the men streaming past. "Panic will only jam the stairs and prevent anyone from escaping. Take it easy."

White-faced men were darting down the steps. Panic glistened wildly in the eyes of a few, but Wentworth's blow had had

41

a sobering effect on them. They went more quietly. Wentworth swung the man he had slugged to his shoulder and they went down. When the man recovered, he set him on his feet and allowed him to make his own way. They had reached the fiftieth floor when a policeman stopped them on the steps.

"All the women out, sir. Three cars waiting here," he reported.

Men jammed toward the door with eager shouts. Wentworth drew a deep breath. They had won that many from the maw of death. He turned tensely to Kirkpatrick.

"You get aboard, Kirk," he said. "You've got to direct that bunch downstairs or they'll be trapped."

KIRKPATRICK SMILED faintly, open-his mouth to speak then shut it again as an abysmal moan of twisted structure beams made deafening noise in the confined stairway. He looked up, watched a hunk of ceiling plaster detach itself and smack to pieces on the floor. When the noise had died, he spoke above the bedlam of terror it caused. His voice was hoarse, tight with enforced calm.

"You're needed, too, Dick," he said quietly. "Don't forget that this is only the beginning of the battle. As usual, I'll be hampered by the confounded laws. We ought to take this Devil Hackerson and torture the truth out of him."

Wentworth pulled up his lip corners with an effort. Death had spoken to all of them in that last groan.

"Quite," he murmured with assumed nonchalance, "Let's recommend it to the Spider."

They went into the hallway and squeezed in behind the last of the men into an already overloaded elevator. They dropped down swiftly. In the lobby, police had formed close-ranked lines and men—all the women had already left—were herded through at a run. If anyone slowed, an officer's nightstick rapped him smartly on the thighs and he speeded up again. The faces of the police were set and grim. Their eyes lifted time and again to the ceilings and the walls that at any moment might come in upon them.

A man ran up to Kirkpatrick. He was in civilian clothes and his face was distraught. "Four main supports of the south side have given away," he reported excitedly. "We can't do a damned thing toward bracing. One more hard gust…" He choked off as a terrific cracking roar thundered through the hall. A crack gaped in the ceiling, then slowly, deliberately, half the mosaic ceiling swung down, hinged at one side, and crashed to the floor. Three men went down under it and police instantly leaped to clear them.

A constant stream of men poured from the elevator banks.

"How many floors to clear?" Kirkpatrick barked.

"Fifteen," the starter shouted.

"Two floors cleared every minute," an officer said curtly beside Kirkpatrick. "Seven more minutes to go. Think it will hold off, sir?"

There was strain in all their voices, a strain they tried to hide. Others had heard that question and many eyes were riveted fearfully, hopefully on the engineer's face.

The engineer shook his head dubiously. "I wouldn't guarantee one minute," he said. "These walls are strong, but it's steel that holds them. When that goes, everything will crumple. And it's going damned fast."

A ringing clang as if a cracked bell of enormous size had been struck gonged hollowly through the building.

"There goes another support," the engineer gasped. He drew out a handkerchief and wiped his forehead. The linen was already soggy perspiration. Kirkpatrick was watching the elevator indicators.

"Have the operators shout at the fifth floor that all below that must walk," he ordered curtly.

A constant stream of white-faced men was belching now from the stairs, the elevators seemed to be moving more swiftly.

"Three floors in the last minute," the officer beside Kirkpatrick reported. "Guess a lot of them have walked down from those floors."

WENTWORTH AND Kirkpatrick stood stiffly side by side as the seconds ticked by and watched the hashing lights which indicated the flight of the elevators. They had worked down to the eighth floor now. One cage dropped to the fifth and stopped, the lights showed, then plunged straight to the main floor. The door yanked open.

"Fifth floor clear!" he shouted.

"All out!" shouted Kirkpatrick. "And run like hell, to the north. This building will flop to the south. All out!"

A dozen voices picked up his cry and two more gonging explosions told that two more girders had crumpled. One by one the elevators swooped to a halt and their operators fled with the passengers. Policemen were ordered out. They tried to keep panic out of their retreat. One broke and ran. Others followed.

Once more Kirkpatrick and Wentworth faced each other.

They nodded. They had done all they could here. They were justified now in trying to save their own lives. They strode swiftly to the door, faces drawn and haggard, turned north amid a stream of other men. The crowd was all ahead of them, pelting away from the danger zone. Wentworth wondered if now, that the work was over, his hand could still hold a flame steadily....

But Wentworth and Kirkpatrick did not run. Wentworth bowed his head into the wind. He was thinking now, with death so close, only a single word, a name, Nita. He did not visualize the woman he loved, did not even think of the death that must soon annihilate him, of the ton of debris that would smear him out of existence. He merely thought her name.

Two blocks away, Wentworth stopped to turn and stare upward at the highest building in the world. As he looked, a shuddering gasp of horror went up from the watching crowd, shivering down on the breath of the icy wind. The building seemed to be leaning. For a moment, it was not possible to tell definitely; then the angle became more pronounced. The tall spire was curved slightly at its middle like a woman's back.

"Run, Dick!" Kirkpatrick barked at him.

"No use, Kirk," Wentworth said heavily. "We couldn't gain more than fifty feet and that wouldn't...."

HE BROKE off, sucking in his breath. The bow in the middle of the building had increased. Wentworth realized that the steel girder had not been applied throughout the building, but only on its major supports. Up there, the beams still held, but it was a useless, futile battle the steel fought with the elements. He saw a speck that was the first huge stone to tear from its seating. He

45

watched it sweep downward, growing larger and larger, saw it strike the roof of a building.

On the top story of that building, the windows burst outward suddenly. Wentworth shook himself. All this was happening in split-seconds, and yet it passed before his lightning swift mind like the movements of a slow-motion camera. His ego seemed to be detached from his body, so that, like a bystander, he watched himself watch this major catastrophe of the world's history that was occurring before his eyes. He realized the millions in damage, knew that hundreds still fought their way downward through nearby buildings and were sprinting up the streets past him toward safety, that other scores could not possibly get free in time.

He felt a stab in his heart that he knew was pain—felt the burn of savage anger in his breast—anger at the madmen who would commit such a fearful deed… A numbness gripped him, too, a numbness like the first shock of a bullet or of grief. He saw a larger section of stone rip loose from the toppling building. Then the mooring mast-tower became detached and somersaulted downward, end over end. It was two hundred feet high and it looked at first like a child's toy. It swooped toward earth, spinning in the wind. It struck in the middle of Fifth Avenue, three blocks south of the Sky Building and exploded into dust. The thunder of its crash billowed up the wide thoroughfare. Windows blew out with the concussion. The moan of the watching crowd was like a dirge.

Now the whole building was disintegrating. It leaned from the base, stately as a forest giant sweeping to destruction. It broke in two places, a third of the way from the top, a third of the way from the bottom. The middle section seemed to move faster than the other two so that the very pinnacle was left for a moment pointing straight upward while the rest of the building pulled away below it. A breath long, that peak poised there, rocks and furnishings streaming from it like blood, a head ripped from a living body.

Then the peak smashed straight downward, struck the falling torso of the Sky Building and splashed stone blood in all directions. With one final cataclysmic wrench, the tons of it fell.

It smeared five city blocks off the face of the earth. It hammered buildings down into the ground, drove them in on their own foundations. It obliterated them.

One huge building stone catapulted twenty blocks, pierced the roof of a subway tunnel and jack-knifed the leading car of an eight-car train. Passengers were pulped. There had been sixty persons in that first car. There was nothing that could be called human in the wreckage.

Wentworth actually saw the building splash its carcass into the street, saw giant jagged blocks of stone that weighed a ton bounce like golf balls. Then the gust of concussion slapped him flat and jarred out his senses.

CHAPTER 5
THE SECOND CALAMITY

THE DARKNESS of unconsciousness lifted like a sullen fog at the insistent demand of Wentworth's will. His struggle jerked at his muscles, made him toss.

"It's all right, Dick." The voice was sweet and deep. He knew that voice, but how had Nita van Sloan got into hell? He gathered all his strength and opened his eyes. He found that he was seated in a car, that it actually was Nita sitting beside him, Nita of the spun-bronze curls and the blue eyes that were like dewy violets. She smiled and Wentworth struggled erect.

"Kirkpatrick?" he questioned.

"He regained consciousness about ten minutes ago," she said. "He's directing the search, of the ruins. He says—" Nita hesitated, and there was a shudder in her voice, "he says at least a thousand were killed and that probably well never know the exact total."

Wentworth nodded slowly, squeezed his temples with his palms. His head felt swollen. Kirkpatrick was right. Anyone in the direct path of those flying building blocks, would he obliterated. Abruptly he thrust himself upward. Nita's hands clung to his arm, then she stood also and climbed out of the car.

"Every building in town must be guarded," Wentworth said, his tongue still moving thickly. As he spoke, his speech and his mind cleared. "There must be an inspection of all steel daily from now on... Where is Kirkpatrick?"

A policeman hurrying past, turned and thrust a rigid arm

toward the south. "In what's left of the building, Sir," he reported. The policeman's face was white and drawn. "But for sweet Mary's sake, don't let the lady go down there. The dead…."

Nita winced as if the man had struck her. "The extras and the radios were crazy with the news of what was happening," she said rapidly. "I heard them and knew you'd be somewhere near. I came down to help, and I'm not going back now."

Wentworth turned his wan face. His mind had fully recovered now, but there was a heavy weakness in his limbs. "You are always brave, my darling," he said to her simply. "But there really is nothing you can do. Wait here until I get Kirkpatrick. I'll be right back."

He insisted and Nita finally climbed into the car to wait. Striding down Fifth Avenue, Wentworth was conscious again of the cold wind whipping against his back, pushing him ahead. There wasn't a whole window along the street. Policeman were on guard against looters everywhere. The cordon had been drawn in since the crash until it extended only five blocks from the wrecked building, but it still barred all entrants except those on official business.

Wentworth was numb to horror now, but he frowned as he was blown on down the street. He could not fathom the motive behind such wanton mass murder. For a moment the idea of looting had brushed his mind, but it was inconceivable that any man could commit such a crime for the sake of petty loot. He would have realized in advance that police would be upon the scene before he could accomplish any sacking. Wentworth's eyes flicked over the scene as he pushed on and his face became haggard.

A stone that weighed a ton had smashed a crater in the street and in its bottom was something viscous and dark, all that was left of a human being. On every side, the Avenue was a shambles. Huddled bodies of men who had not been struck were crushed against jagged cracked walls, broken by the force of the concussion. Entire sides of buildings had been driven in. Southward, the city looked like a thrice-bombed town of Flanders. Scarcely two bricks had been left atop each other. It spread over entire blocks. Just how far, it was hard to estimate, for it was no longer possible to make out where the cross streets had been.

IN THE midst of the ruins, Wentworth found Kirkpatrick and told him rapidly what he thought should be done. Kirkpatrick nodded at once and issued the orders.

"I've put out an alarm for Devil Hackerson," he said curtly. "The Collins have left their apartment in Middleton and gave no address. Their home-town down South hasn't heard from them. What other trails are there to follow?"

"I'll question Ram Singh," said Wentworth slowly. "Chemists are analyzing the broken steel, of course?"

NITA VAN SLOAN

Kirkpatrick nodded, turned aside to give some instructions to an inspector who came up hurriedly. Abruptly the three men reeled, staggered and brought up sprawling over a pile of debris. Wentworth scrambled erect and stared northward. Billows of dust were racing down the wind. The earth trembled beneath them and a roar like ten thousand Niagaras dinned in their ears.

Wentworth's keen eyes swept the skyline northward and his fists knotted at his sides. He ground out a curse that hurt his throat.

"God in heaven, Kirk!" he said, his voice scarcely more than a whisper. "Can you—can you see the Plymouth spire?"

Kirkpatrick seized his arm and the fingers ate into Wentworth's flesh like steel talons. "It isn't possible, Dick," he rasped. "They can't… can't…!"

A motorcycle rocketed down the Avenue, dodging the holes that pitted it like shell craters. The policeman yanked the machine to a halt, leaped from it and raced the last fifty yards flat-footed. He ran with his head thrown back, his face twisted by horror, his eyes staring. He pounded up and Kirkpatrick seized his shoulders. The officer opened his mouth, swallowed, finally squeezed out words.

"Plymouth building, sir," he gasped. "She… she…!"

The inadequacy of words seemed to choke the man. He raised an arm rigid over his head and swished it down, struck a gloved hand flat into another. He nodded his head.

"The Plymouth building fell," he said flatly. "Grand Central went, too…."

Wentworth felt his lips skin back from his teeth, knew that he shouted hoarse meaningless sounds from his throat, felt the white flame of consuming fury rise within him. By God, when the Spider found the man behind this, he would grind him to death beneath his heels! The Plymouth building and the Grand

Central station destroyed! Grand Central station where thousands poured into the city daily! More blocks of the city laid to waste, pulverized by tons of steel and masonry piling down from incredible heights.

A thousand had died in the crash of the Sky Building despite police warning and frantic efforts to clear the surrounding area. *And up there in the Plymouth building, there had been no warning!*

Imagination reeled beneath the shock. There would be thousands, literally thousands who would never again be heard from, whose families would never know their fate. And it would be better so. Wentworth thought of that pit in the street with its dark, viscous pool. A shudder swept him. He was trembling all over, his muscles jerking and quivering. Slowly he fought himself to calmness. Kirkpatrick had gasped a few orders that had sent police to the scene of disaster.

Slowly, a cold rage swept the horror from Wentworth's breast. He turned a graven, bitter face to Kirkpatrick.

"Better clear the whole area of skyscrapers of people," he said, and he could scarcely recognize his own voice. "Keep it clear until inspections can be finished. Better call on some expert in skyscraper mechanics to help."

Kirkpatrick nodded. "Good God in heaven," he whispered. "I hope the Spider and not myself gets these fiends. The Spider won't have to use civilized methods of punishment."

Wentworth nodded. He slowly took out his cigarette case and offered it to Kirkpatrick and the Police Commissioner's fingers shook. Wentworth's hand was like rock. He felt that his heart was like that, too, cold and hard. He lighted a cigarette.

"I think, Kirk," he said calmly, "that you can count on that."

RESOLUTELY, WENTWORTH drove all shock and horror from his brain as he strode back up Fifth Avenue to where Nita waited for him, huddled in furs in her small coupé. A glance at his face told her that he knew what had happened, that he was intent on plans, and she drove southward without a word, circling to the west around the area of shattered buildings and streets. The traffic congestion stalled them for long minutes and they deserted the car for an elevated train, walked across town to Wentworth's apartment.

The private elevator to his penthouse shot them upward fifteen floors, and the door swung open as they crossed the hall. The ruddy face of old Jenkyns, the butler, was creased with smiles as he ducked his crown of white hair in a profound bow. He always greeted Nita thus. It was his fondest hope that some day his master would marry and cease these mad adventures of his—these quixotic tilts with crime.

Wentworth did not speak. He stalked past his butler, across the living room with its stone fireplace and smoky beams into the music-room beyond. Within the door, he stopped. He heard Nita behind him and turned to face her, a slow, grave smile moving his lips. Nita came close into his arms, pressed her bronze curls against his breast. In her heart was sadness, too. She knew that Wentworth had pledged himself ever to battle the underworld, ever to right the crooked wrongs that afflicted humanity. Right now, she was not sorry. This was a crusade she would not have the Spider shirk.

But there was sadness within her, too. She knew how both

of them had fought their love because the Spider could never marry—how could the Spider marry and build a home, have a family, when he knew not what day the police would clap vengeful hands upon his shoulders and send him to his death as a common murderer?—but their love had proved stronger than even the Spider's grim power.

In the end, Nita, too, had taken the pledge of service with which Wentworth had bound himself. It was their only pleasure that they fought side by side through death and horror. Something of all this was flitting through Wentworth's brain as he clasped her close in his arms, smiling grimly above her head into the empty blackness beyond his windows which formerly had framed the majesty of the Sky Building. He was remembering, too, what horror had faced Nita in his last battle with the underworld, when she had so narrowly escaped a fearful death.*

The smile squeezed off his mouth. If that fiendish Chinese, Wu Chang, had been a ruthless enemy, this present monster must be the chief ruler of Hell!

He led Nita gently to a chair and strode across to the end of the room where a mighty organ had been installed. Waiting only

---

* AUTHOR'S NOTE: The Author refers here to the Spider's battle with the fiendish Chinese Wu Chang and his cold-blooded, though beautiful daughter Ya Che, in which Nita was seized by the Chinese in an attempt to force Wentworth to assist in their nefarious plans. They imprisoned Nita in a steel-barred cell and then let into her prison an orang-outang, whose mate they intended she should become. These adventures were narrated in that adventure of the Spider which Mr. Stockbridge called "The Red Death Rain."

to toss his overcoat aside, Wentworth seated himself before the instrument, manipulated the stops and began to play. His music was extemporaneous; its chords crashed with thunder like the collapse of the Sky Building. Its theme mounted in wild wind-like fury. Nita sank back in her chair and closed her eyes. She knew that her Dick found in music a release that nothing else could afford. She knew that his mind was tortured by the sufferings of the thousands, in this latest mad raid of the underworld on civilization, that he sought to calm himself so that he might think more clearly.

On and on thundered the soaring notes, the crashing basses. Jenkyns brought in a tray upon which decanter and syphon stood, and stepped back against the wall, his ruddy old face distraught. He, too, knew the black despair which spoke through the music. Another form stepped into the doorway. Ram Singh, clad in spotless white, his head wrapped in a fresh turban that strengthened the hard, clean mold of his features, pale now with pain. His left arm was strapped to his body. His eyes, dog-like with devotion, fastened on Wentworth and he, too, waited.

THEY WAITED long. It was an hour before the mad, vaulting chords gave way to gentler strains, another half hour before they droned into the sweeping phases of love music. And Nita knew now that Wentworth played to her. The tension that had gripped her relaxed. She let her wrists go limp upon the chair arms. Her eyes strayed over the beauty of the room, touched the Steinway concert grand, the Stradivarius violin that was Wentworth's special joy. The music of the organ died in a lingering quaver, and it was the old alert Wentworth who spun from the bench, strode energetically across the room.

His eyes spotted Ram Singh. "Damn your fighting soul, Ram Singh," he grinned. "Why don't you stay in the hospital when you're sick?"

Ram Singh's eyes gleamed into his master's. "Pooh. It is nothing." He slapped his wounded shoulder with his good right hand. "A mere pin prick. I knew you would need me."

Wentworth stopped before him, standing on straddled legs. A tenseness touched his eyes. "Did you find Hackerson's headquarters?" he asked.

Ram Singh stiffened like a soldier at attention. "I traced him to a saloon, *Sahib,*" he reported. "There he talked with one who was bald-headed and had a cast in his left eye. Hackerson addressed him as Baldy. Baldy asked if the Sky Building had been fixed so it would collapse and Hackerson said it had. I left at once to report, but they must have seen me. I was shot down even as I began to tell you about it." He recounted then what had been said in the automobile while he was being carried to the Sky Building to die—of Baldy's words of the Master, of the anonymous "stuff" that had been put on the steel girders.

"Describe this bald man," Wentworth asked softly, and listened with narrowed eyes while Ram Singh told how he looked. He shook his head at the end. "I never heard of such a criminal," he said. "Go to police headquarters and see if you can find him in the rogue's gallery. If you identify him, tell *Sahib* Kirkpatrick what you have told me." He nodded in dismissal and Ram Singh backed three paces, raised his cupped hand to his turbaned forehead in a salaam, pivoted and was gone.

Jenkyns announced dinner, and Wentworth noted with surprise that the mad day had faded. He had not eaten since the night before. Knowing that he must battle soon, he allowed himself an hour more with Nita, during which time they ate the perfect meal Jenkyns had prepared.

Back in the living room, Wentworth took a turn up and down, paused before Nita. "Darling, will you get in touch with Professor Brownlee and have him install an infra-red camera in the Collins apartment in Middleton? And, darling…!" He paused, smiling down at her tenderly. "Hide yourself at some hotel. I'm afraid these killers may strike at me through you."

He bent over her, a hand on each arm of her chair, brushed her gleaming hair with his lips. Nita lifted her mouth to his, pressed her soft cheek to his with closed eyes. Wentworth's arms dropped about her shoulders, tightened savagely. It was as if he would shield her with that moment's caress from all the fury of the world, the madness of criminal onslaughts. When he released her, his eyes were gentle.

"It may be some days before I see you again, dear," he said briskly. "There is much to do."

He saw rebellious protest on Nita's face and promised swiftly that he had work for her, too, but that first he must make certain investigations…. Then he sent her away. Five minutes later he was driving away in his town sedan, the Lancia in which he had burned the roads between Middleton and New York. In a dark side street, he parked and drew the curtains, entered the tonneau.

His hand dropped to a button beneath the left half of the cushion and that section slid forward and revolved soundlessly.

It's back contained clothing hung on racks and from it Wentworth unfolded a mirror and make-up tray framed with mazdas. He went to work swiftly. Beneath his skillful hands the face of Richard Wentworth became sallow and sharp, the nose lengthened and bushy black brows that were low over his eyes masked the mockery of his own smooth eyebrows. A lank, black wig, a broad-brimmed hat of black and a cape completed the transformation. He pocketed false celluloid teeth like fangs. Again Richard Wentworth had become the Spider. He climbed slowly from the tonneau, and shuffling along the walk, he was a hunchback, twisted shoulders distorting the smooth erect stride that was Wentworth's.

THE SPIDER'S face was set and hard. Tonight he was borrowing a leaf from the book of gangsterdom. It dictated that when you could not find the man you wanted, you attacked where it would hurt that man. The police would be before him, of course, watching for Hackerson to fall into their hands. But Wentworth would not wait....

He turned around a corner, his cape flapping behind him in the cold whip of the wind, a somber, half-seen shadow in the swift-falling winter dusk, and saw a block ahead the apartment house where lived Beatrice Ross, Devil Hackerson's mistress. As he shuffled closer, he made out the forms of two men hidden in a facing doorway. His lips stirred slightly in mockery. The police were watching for Hackerson, waiting for him to drop into their laps. As if Hackerson, knowing that police and the Spider both were upon his trail, would walk openly into so obvious a place as his mistress' home!

Wentworth circled the block to avoid the detectives, for his hunched and caped figure was known throughout the land as the disguise of the Spider. He turned alongside the apartment house where Hackerson's girl friend lived, moved close within the shadow of the wall. A black stairway opened downward, tunneling under the next building. Wentworth drifted into it soundlessly, brought up against a steel grating. A lock pick disposed of that in seconds and he moved through into a black areaway walled in by the towering, window-pierced cliffs of apartment houses.

Two minutes later, he was moving steadily up the stairs of the Beatrice Ross' house. He reached the fourth floor without challenge, paused a moment outside the door that bore the bronze figures *4C*. The lock brought a small smile to his lips. Hackerson would know the best kind to use all right. A Foxx. It was a tough nut to crack. A glance showed him the fire-escape exit on his right. He reached the window in quick, quiet strides, slid outside. From the platform, it was only a long step to the sill of the woman's bathroom window. That would be the bedroom that was lighted next to it.

Without hesitation, Wentworth stepped across four stories of deep blackness to the sill, crouched there while a cold wind flapped his cloak dully behind him. The window slid up noiselessly and slipping into place his false celluloid fangs, he crept inside, stepping on a steam radiator that hissed dimly, then to the floor. Abruptly the light snapped on, smashing into his eyes.

A woman stood in the doorway with an automatic in her hand. "So what do you want, baby?" she sneered. "Come out and show your ugly mug."

Evidently she had started to undress. Her long hennaed hair hung down her naked left shoulder and her clothing consisted of a magenta silken underskirt and, above the waist, nothing but a narrow brassier that compressed her ample breasts. Her undress did not appear to concern her.

"Come on, baby," she urged, mocking. "Come out where mama can see you better."

Wentworth saw that her lips were brilliantly carmined and their sullen curve was hard as brass. He came forward two slow steps, bared those ugly, inch-long fangs, and lifted his head so that the light crept in under the broad brim of his hat. The woman gasped, retreated a step. Her gun hand began to waver, and then she seized the automatic with both hands and jerked it eye high.

"*The Spider! The Spider!*" she gabbled and began shooting.

CHAPTER 6
THE HOT TRAIL

WENTWORTH HAD counted on the woman's fright. He dived in under the gun an instant before she yanked the trigger. His shoulder caught the woman's ankles and spilled her across his back. He heard the gun smash into a mirror, heard the woman's frightened shriek. Her head thudded against the edge of the wash bowl. Wentworth scrambled up, and the woman crouched on hands and knees, head hanging, swaying from side to side like an injured animal. The rest of her hair had come down and its dyed and lifeless ends swept the floor.

Wentworth seized her shoulders, dragged her erect and pinned her against the wall. Her mouth was sagging open, her eyes barely showed the irises. She was half out, but a dashing of water from the bowl jerked her back to full consciousness. He thrust his face, the sallow, menacing face of the Spider, close to hers; his lips snarled back from pointed fangs.

"You're going with me," he snapped, "and you're going fast— or you're going out feet first. Which will it be?"

The woman's over-red mouth gagged. She shook her head in bewilderment.

"Police are at the door," Wentworth said, emphasizing his words with a violent shake of her shoulders. "Either come with me or I drop you right here." He dragged out his gun and stabbed its muzzle against her abdomen. "I—I'll go," she whimpered.

Wentworth led her into the next room, snatched a coat from a closet and threw it at her, and she got into it with fumbling hands. He listened at the door, then hurried her through it to the hall beyond. They went down the fire-escape while police were coming up in the elevator, dived through the passageway that a steel grating closed and moments later reached Wentworth's car. The woman huddled in the opposite corner. The winter night bit through her and her lips beneath the carmine were purple with cold. She watched the Spider with cringing eyes.

Wentworth apparently paid her no attention. The woman

He kicked in the window and went in guns first.

hugged herself for warmth. "Where—where are you taking me?" she asked.

Wentworth skated to the curb and twisted his long-nosed face toward her.

"Nowhere," he said softly. "You're taking me to Devil Hackerson, or else—" He let his voice trail off and the flat mocking laughter of the Spider filled the car.

The woman shivered and huddled miserably in her corner. "He'd—he'd kill me."

"Probably," Wentworth agreed carelessly. "Start talking."

Stark fright was on the face. She stammered out a hoarse plea for mercy, but her voice was hopeless. Wentworth took out his automatic slowly and once more the ugly mirth of the Spider spilled from his lips. Beatrice Ross whimpered.

"Get out," Wentworth ordered.

"No, no!"

"Then take it here!" Wentworth presented the gun. The woman's hands clawed at him desperately, snatching at the weapon. Wentworth cursed and jerked open his door, backed out. Beatrice Ross scrambled out the opposite side and began to run with crazy frightened shrieks. The Spider raised his gun deliberately, squeezed off a bullet.

"Oh, God!" The woman stumbled, clapped a hand to her shoulder.

A mirthless smile twisted Wentworth's lips. He had merely burned the flesh. He fired another bullet and fragments of cement stung her ankles. As she went around the corner, Wentworth blew chips off the bricks, then sprang to his car and spurted away. He circled the block in time to see the woman almost fall into a taxi. With a smooth twist of the wheel, the Spider took up the trail he hoped would lead to Devil Hackerson....

THE TAXI droned southward on Riverside Drive, took the elevated highway along the Hudson shore and slanted down a vamp at 19th Street. It stopped at the entrance of a huge apartment house that sprawled over two blocks, one of those "colonies" that have sprung up among the tenements of New York's east and west sides to take care of the mounting demand for modern apartment quarters convenient to the business districts. The hallboy stared at the badge that Wentworth showed and stammered out that the woman had gone to Apartment 305.

The Spider was smiling as the elevator lifted him. If he knew Hackerson, the man would have assured himself of at least two exits to his apartment. That meant it would be on a fire-escape. Within two minutes after he reached the third floor, Wentworth confirmed his guess. He stood on the steel lattice-work of the fire-escape outside an apartment whose shades were drawn. He heard excited voices within.

"It was the Spider, I tell you," Beatrice Ross was blurting. "He tried to make me tell where you were and I wouldn't, then he said he was going to kill me. I ran and he shot at me three times, but didn't hit me."

Wentworth laughed silently. Even as he had hoped, the woman had fled straight to Devil Hackerson.

"You damned fool!" a man choked. "You damned fool! Do you think the Spider could shoot three times and miss? He just wanted you to come here so he could follow. You lousy little—" the sound of a sodden blow came through the closed window—"little tramp!"

Beatrice Ross's sobs filled the room.

"Butts," the man snapped. "Dig out and scout around the building. Muggsie, keep watch in the hall. I'll sit tight and wait. The Spider will be here any minute."

There was a silence of moments broken only by the sobbing of the woman. "It wasn't nothing like that, Devil," she pleaded. "I know it wasn't. I wouldn't fall for a sappy move like that. He shot at me and missed. He burned my shoulder once—"

"Shut up," Hackerson growled. "I want to hear the Spider when he comes. My God, *the fire-escape!* It isn't covered!"

Wentworth smiled thinly. He kicked in the window and the shade snapped up. He went in guns first and caught Hackerson half out of his chair, hand going for rod too late.

"Yes, Hackerson, the fire-escape," said Wentworth quietly, "but you were a little slow in thinking about it." The sinister flat laughter of the Spider filled the room.

DEVIL HACKERSON'S hand quivered at his vest opening, but he could not make up his mind to go for his gun, not with the Spider's two automatics leveled on his breast, not with the Spider's glacial eyes boring into him. The woman on the floor whimpered and moaned. She clasped her hands before her and rose straight on her knees and swayed backward and forward. Her coat came open and her brassier had slipped. Her hair was wild about her shoulders. She didn't say a word, just moaned.

Hackerson was unconsciously backing. His knees struck the

davenport and he dropped down on the cushions and bounced soggily. The tip of his tongue touched his lips.

"What do you want?" he asked hoarsely.

"First," said the Spider, his fantastic fanged teeth chopping off the words. "First, the name of the man who ordered that job on the Plymouth and the Sky buildings."

Hackerson sucked in a deep breath. His eyes were riveted with hypnotic fascination on Wentworth's gaze.

"For God's sake, don't shoot, Spider," he whispered. "I don't know."

"What about Baldy?" The words were little more than a hiss. Wentworth was listening for other things than the moaning of the woman and Hackerson's reply. He was listening for the possible return of Butts and Muggsie. They had been ordered to prowl outside, but they might return. If Butts peered up at the window and saw the curtains flapping out into the frigid night, he might think it worth investigating.

"What about Baldy?" Wentworth asked and Hackerson's eyes widened in surprise. "How do you reach Baldy?"

"I don't," Hackerson protested hoarsely, and winced. Wentworth had made no move, but cold lights flamed in the Spider's eyes "I don't get in touch with him," Hackerson spoke hurriedly. "He always seems to know where to reach me whether I'm at home or in a restaurant or wherever I am. He brings the stuff and he brings the money, and that's all I know."

"What's the 'stuff' like?" Wentworth was disappointed, blocked in this lead through which he had hoped to trace the man Baldy and his Master. But he believed Hackerson told the truth. It confirmed what Ram Singh's story had indicated, the anonymity of the Master.

"Jeez, Spider," Hackerson whined, "he'll rub me out if I spill all this to you."

Wentworth cursed, and Hackerson broke off, a yelp of fear in his throat as Wentworth stepped forward.

He took only a single stride toward Hackerson, then seemed to trip and go flat down on the floor. He rolled on his right side and flame leaped from both guns toward the window. A black figure there reeled to its feet, mouth opened in a soundless scream. Butts, Wentworth saw, was accounted for. He hurled upward to his knees, caught Hackerson as the man pulled his gun clear. He saw Beatrice Ross on her feet plunging toward him and dodged as his left gun spat. He failed to get clear and the woman's charge sprawled him sideways to the floor. She fell upon him, sobbing and fighting. Fingernails tore at his face, knees drummed his side. He swept his right arm in a swishing semi-circle and the woman slapped down hard on the floor, her feet thrashing. She was up like a cat, leaping toward him with fingers clawing.

Wentworth cursed angrily. A fragmentary glance showed him that Hackerson was out of the fight at least for a time, slumped down on the davenport, but Muggsie would crash in at any moment, drawn by the shots. A short upward jar of his gun and Beatrice Ross sat down again. Her legs were straddled out, her arms braced sideways on the floor. Her mouth sagged. **WENTWORTH WHIRLED,** his quick glance sweeping the room. He saw the door whip open, saw Muggsie charge in with his revolver leaping at his side, spewing lead. A bullet jerked at Wentworth's hat, a second nipped the lobe of his ear, then Muggsie reeled against the door jamb and went down under a blast of Spider lead. Wentworth jerked back to Hackerson, cursed violently.

Hackerson was dead, a bullet through the base of his throat. The Spider's sure aim had been directed at the right shoulder, intended only to cripple the man so that he still could reveal the secrets of the Master or be used as bait for Baldy. The woman's attack had jerked his gun in the instant of discharge—and killed Hackerson.

Excited shouts were ringing through the corridors. A woman shrieked for police in a high, frightened voice. Wentworth bounded to the door, yanked Muggsie's body inside, stooped to print his seal on the man's forehead. A moment he paused also beside each of the other bodies to leave his crimson sinister signature. The woman had reeled to her feet now, stood swaying.

"By God, Spider," she swore. "I'll get you for this, you…" Her voice spewed filthy abuse. She staggered toward him, tears streaming down her face, wetting the cheek that still bore the crimson imprint of Hackerson's blow. Wentworth pushed her aside, held her off with a hand on her shoulder while she leaned forward, swiping at him futilely.

"You can give a message to Baldy," the Spider said, slowly. "You tell him this is just a token payment. Tell him I shall kill every hireling of his Master, himself included, on sight. The Spider will show no more mercy. From now on, he will kill! *kill! KILL!*"

He thrust Beatrice Ross away and she reeled with arms swinging wildly. Wentworth stepped to the fire-escape, swung rapidly downward. He heard the Ross woman screeching from the window. Flame lanced from her hand and gun-noise racketed in the narrow areaway. But her bullets only clanged off the steel framework of the fire-escape and splatted against the concrete floor of the areaway.

As he dashed through the hallways of another of the colony buildings, a white-faced man stepped into his path with a gun in a trembling hand. A swift blow sent the gun scaling along the floor and the Spider went out into the street. The eerie shriek of police sirens was close at hand, but he reached his car before the first of the radio patrol-cars skated into the street. His eyes, as he drove quietly away, were burning points of flame. His only accomplishment had been to wipe out the one tangible clue he had to the Master. There remained—Beatrice Ross.

CHAPTER 7
LULL BEFORE THE STORM

A S WENTWORTH drove on, a cold smile touched his lips. The fiery action had cooled his rage, left only the steel-like bite of avenging anger. He swerved to the curb, called police headquarters and got Ram Singh on the telephone.

"Have you had any success, Ram Singh?" he queried.

The Hindu's voice was expressionless, but there was weariness behind it. "There is not a picture in the Rogue's gallery like the man I saw."

"Very well, I have another task for thee, Ram Singh," Wentworth lapsed into staccato Hindustani, for he did not know who might be listening upon the wire. "Devil Hackerson is dead with the seal of the Spider upon his forehead. Police will bring in presently a woman known as Beatrice Ross. When she is freed, follow her and before many hours, you should meet again your friend, Baldy. When you do, drop the woman and trail the man. Report through Jenkyns."

He parked his car and speedily stripped off the disguise of the Spider, becoming then a blond young man with full cheeks and a bristling, reddish mustache. He exaggerated his customary erect stride as he entered the Kennillworth Hotel on Forty-Sixth Street. He walked with an accentuated tap of heels, a slight sway of the left hip that cavalrymen everywhere would recognize, the stride of an officer accustomed to wearing spurs and swaying the dangling saber out of the way of his booted calves.

At the desk, his incisive question revealed that Anse Collins' room was on the eleventh floor. Wentworth crossed to a house phone to talk with him, and the clerk scowled after him. These army men were all like that, so used to service by others that they never had a courteous word for anyone.

"Collins," Wentworth said softly as the man answered the phone, "this is the man you have been expecting. I'll be right up."

"Good!" Collins snapped. "I was getting ready to go out on my own. I'm thinking that the same thing that was used to break that safe caused these buildings to fall today."

Wentworth found that Nancy Collins had a room down the hall from her brother-in-law. "If you don't mind," the deputy

71

said, "I reckon we don't need to bother Nancy any. She's had a powerful tough time of it lately." His eyes were keenly studying Wentworth's face, skipped over the brownish tweeds he had donned. "I reckon I wouldn't know you."

A broad smile curved Wentworth's lips. "Probably not," he agreed. There were few persons in the world more adept at disguise than the Spider. It was not that he changed his face radically. It was simply that with each new identity went an entirely new personality. He spoke differently, walked with a distinct stride, carried head and shoulders as would the man whose character he had assumed. He pushed on without a pause in his conversation.

"There's work to be done, Collins, if you want to get the man who was responsible for your brother's death."

"You mean Hackerson?" The deputy's words were slow, but there was a thin white thin line around his compressed mouth.

Wentworth shook his head shortly. "Not Hackerson. I killed him less than a half-hour ago."

Coffins' eyes jerked wide, then narrowed. "You're pretty open about it, Mr. Spider," he said slowly. "How do you know I'm not going to turn you over to the police?"

"That would be a poor way to repay a friend's help," Wentworth smiled at him quietly. "And down where you come from, men usually stick by their friends."

"That's right, by God!" Collins' voice took on a rough edge. "And we remember our enemies, too!"

WENTWORTH GLANCED down at the man's fists. They were small in proportion to his size, but they would carry the enormous powers of those shoulders, that deep chest. He took in the strong face and the rumpled brown hair. Apparently, it was always like that, tousled as if from sleeping. A comb wouldn't do much to it. A woman would love to run her fingers through it....

"Here's the job," Wentworth said swiftly. "I want you to offer yourself as bait to an attack by the criminals. It's pretty clear that they think you have information about the chemicals your brother devised. We'll go to Middleton together and see if we can draw their fire. Frankly, I haven't a clue to the identities of the men behind this business. I didn't want to kill Hackerson until after he had answered some questions, but he went for his gun and I had to."

Collins nodded, frowning. "That listens good to me, but I don't like to hear you say you've got no clue. As sure as you're a foot high, that guy DeHaven Alrecht has got something to do with this."

"That's one of the reasons I'm going to Middleton," Wentworth told him. "I want to have a little private conversation with that gentlemen and also with this Bill Butterworth who worked with your brother."

"Butterworth has gone away somewhere," Collins said. His eyes were thoughtful. He pulled aside the left half of his vest and tugged out a smooth-worn forty-four.

"She's a mite short," he said, spinning the chamber, "but I find she comes out quicker like this." He shoved the gun back, patted the butt "When do we start?"

"In the morning," Wentworth told him. "In the meantime, I'd

73

like you to identify yourself to Police Commissioner Kirkpatrick. It's possible you might be able to help him some."

Collins snapped his fingers. "By golly, I knew there was something we had to tell you," he said. "Before you busted in at Middleton, there was another guy there. You had to leave so quickly we couldn't tell you. This guy asked some questions, then seemed to get scared when Hackerson was talking about hurting us if we didn't talk. He beat it then."

Wentworth's eyes keened. "A bald man?" he asked quickly, "with a cast in his left eye?"

Collins nodded slowly, his eyes wonderingly on Wentworth's face. "I reckon you know everything, Mr. Spider," he said slowly. "That's the guy."

"Good," Wentworth's head came up joyfully. "You and Mrs. Collins go down to the police and give them the best description you can of that man. This is the first time witnesses have been found against him. I'll come by for you in the morning and we'll go to Middleton. Maybe we'll have luck."

"Maybe," Collins agreed. He was grinning. "Say, man, I'd like to shake hands with you. You're my sort of folks, Mr. Spider."

Wentworth gripped Collins' hand firmly. "Just call me Spider," he laughed. "Your mister sounds too formal."

Collins laughed also, strode down the hall with Wentworth. The Spider didn't wait to see Nancy. He wanted to be at police headquarters when they got there and he had to rid himself of the disguise in the meantime. He had to find this man, Baldy, and make him talk. Wentworth's face set hard. He'd make the man talk, or kill him. Then, perhaps, he could force the Master to show his hand, to battle in the open. So far it had all been movements of pawns. The Master had delivered several telling strokes, but he still had not revealed the purposes behind his attack. Wentworth felt that if he could learn that motive, he might have a better chance of reaching the Master himself.

THE CRIMINAL leader was undoubtedly very clever. He had not appeared at all himself—had worked only through this strange, timid mouthpiece, Baldy. He used gangs of known criminals with whom he never came in contact. From Ram Singh's account of Hackerson's conversation with Baldy, it seemed that even the mouthpiece did not know the Master. It was a damned clever organization. It meant that the man had all the underworld at his service without himself being identified with it in any way. No matter how many of his hirelings Wentworth wiped out, there would always be more on tap. The Master himself would have to be found before these wholesale slaughterings could be stopped.

It was the old alert Wentworth who strode into police head-quarters, buoyant of step, a stiff, slightly arrogant poise to his shapely head, an erect athletic swing of shoulders that bespoke the muscular strength beneath the superb tailoring of his clothing. Kirkpatrick saw him at once. A small alert man sat beside his desk, smoking a big cigar that seemed incongruous with his van Dyke and imperial mustaches. He bounded to his feet, pumped Wentworth's hand energetically as Kirkpatrick introduced them.

"W. Johnson Briggs?" Wentworth inquired and the man nodded, bit out a quick assent. "Yes, yes, of course. W. Johnson

75

Briggs. And you're Richard Wentworth, of course." He laughed, jabbed the wet end of his fuming cigar at Kirkpatrick, shoved it back in his mouth again. "This man wants to know how you can stop steel from caving in. How you can save buildings even if steel crystallizes. Damned nonsense, of course. There isn't any way."

Wentworth smiled at the machine gun chatter of the little man. The cigar was locked between his teeth, billowing smoke up in front of his face. There were four chewed butts on the desk. W. Johnson Briggs was one of the country's biggest consultant architects on skyscrapers. Kirkpatrick had done well to call in a man who knew his craft so thoroughly. Wentworth scrutinized him curiously. The man had an aesthetic face, wore his hair long and swept back over his ears. He chewed and puffed his cigar at the same time.

Kirkpatrick said grimly, "We've got to find a way, Mr. Briggs. Got to! We can't keep the city crippled as it is now. We've got guards to prevent anyone entering the skyscrapers and even the Mayor is howling at me about it. Inspectors are going over the buildings as fast as they can, but it's slow work.

They all three looked up quickly as a policeman opened the door, thrust in a head of carroty bristles. "Guy named Collins out here. Commissioner," he said. "Says he's got some evidence for you. Got a lady with him."

Kirkpatrick's face was interested. "That must be those people from Middleton," he told Wentworth. "Show them in at once."

Collins' face was flushed when he came through the door behind Nancy Collins. He glared at the policeman who shut the door. Wentworth hid a smile behind the lighting of a cigarette. It was hard to get through to Kirkpatrick if the police didn't know you. The big deputy strode forward purposefully.

"I'm Anse Collins, sir," he said to Kirkpatrick, half-turned as Nancy came forward. "And this is my brother's... my brother's widow."

Kirkpatrick bowed gravely, came around the desk to place a chair for Mrs. Collins, and introduced Wentworth and Briggs. There was a tightness upon Nancy's pretty face that did not belong there and the smudges beneath her eyes were purple shadows. Her blue eyes rose hesitantly to Kirkpatrick's face.

"You know who we are?" she asked softly.

"You come from Middleton?" Kirkpatrick queried, and at her nod he said that he knew, then, who they were.

"The Spider saved us from some men in Middleton," Nancy said. Her voice was softened by a drawl. She was looking at her hands in her lap now, fingering a handkerchief. "The police there wouldn't believe that Jim..." Her hands gripped tightly together and she went on, "that Jim was murdered. But the Spider did. Tonight he came to our hotel and told us we ought to come and tell you all we know."

"By Judas Priest!" exploded Briggs. "Listen at the calm way she says it. Just like the Spider was anybody else. He came to our hotel, she says." He shoved the cigar into his mouth and puffed vigorously. Nancy Collins looked up at him and smiled slightly. Her lips were full, a little tremulous. "He was... very nice," she said gently. "And he believed me when I told him about Jim."

"He's all right, that Spider fellow," Anse Collins put in shortly.

"He may be a killer, but he's the real goods. Those rats he killed tonight needed killing."

KIRKPATRICK EYED him keenly. "That couldn't possibly be in the newspapers yet," he said. "So I guess it was the Spider who talked to you all right. He told you he killed Hackerson?"

Collins' eyes narrowed. "Maybe I'd better not say," he replied cautiously. "I'm not saying anything might hurt the Spider. Hell!" the word was explosive, "I shook hands with him."

Wentworth nodded his head slowly, leaned back in his chair. He knew now what he had come to learn. He had wanted to know how far he could trust this Anse Collins and the man was, as he himself had put it, the real goods. He listened without comment while Nancy Collins and her brother-in-law told about Baldy and said they could identify him. Kirkpatrick had her go into details on the description, nodding now and then as it checked with Ram Singh's word picture.

"He's new to the criminal world," Kirkpatrick said finally. "But we're hoping to hear about him soon."

Wentworth knew what that meant. Every detective in headquarters would have his stool pigeons scurrying about, seeking trace of this queer bald-headed man with a cast in one eye who brought the orders of wholesale murder from the Master. They might find out something that way, but it was Wentworth's guess the men the Master hired would be too well paid to talk and that they would shield Baldy from all impudent inquiries—with murder if necessary.

He looked up sharply at an angrily defiant note in Collins' voice.

"Nancy didn't see him, and you won't get it out of me if you keep me in jail from now to Judgment Day," he declared and his tousled head was in that defiant posture that Wentworth was coming to find familiar. "I shook hands with the Spider and I'm for him."

"Good boy!" Briggs applauded. Wentworth saw that he was standing beside Nancy Collins now. The woman was smiling up at him. "Stand by your guns!"

Kirkpatrick smiled thinly, but there was sympathy on his saturnine face. He touched his mustache with thumb and fore-finger, hiding the lifting of his mouth corners.

"I suspect there are many who feel as you do right now," he said slowly. "There are times when I'd like to strike as surely and directly as the Spider does in exacting punishment on evil doers. This man he killed tonight, Hackerson, was directly responsible for the collapse of the Sky Building."

Wentworth left the commissioner's office with a warm feeling in his chest, found Nita at the hotel to which she had gone and insisted on her going to a late supper with him at the Waldorf. According to what Ram Singh had reported, the Master knew that Ram Singh was the servant of the Spider; that probably meant he knew Wentworth's identity, too. Perhaps, the Master would attack....

He was warily watchful as he returned to his apartment and dressed, but nothing suspicious occurred. Jenkyns had not heard from Ram Singh, but Professor Brownlee—once Wentworth's science professor at college, now his devoted friend and helper— had reported that the infrared camera was installed in the

Collins' Middleton apartment. Wentworth was out again within ten minutes, lounging behind the competent broad shoulders of his chauffeur Jackson, who wove the Lancia through traffic with insolent ease.

Halfway to Nita's hotel, Jackson leaned to the speaking tube. "I think we're being followed, Major. That yellow taxi has been behind us the whole way and every other car has passed us."

"Quite right, Jackson," Wentworth told him, with a hard eagerness in his voice. "I had spotted it." Jackson called him Major because he had served under Wentworth in France.

He continued to lounge carelessly in his seat. This would make it necessary for Nita to change her quarters again, of course, but he might inveigle the trailers into an earlier attack. He frowned as the yellow taxi cut a corner and left them, but within the next half dozen blocks, he was equally sure that a Ford coupé was on their trail.

Nita awaited him in the lounge and more than one man turned his head as they strolled toward the street again. There was envy in their stares, perhaps wistfulness. It was so patent that these two had eyes only for each other. It was clear in the way Nita's hand rested confidently on Wentworth's arm, in the eagerness with which her bright laugh met his whispered words.

But Wentworth was not talking love words. "I'm being followed, darling," he whispered. "Let's hope we get a shot at the Master himself tonight."

And Nita's laughter was clever camouflage. "I'm getting to be a good gun moll," she told him. "I've got an automatic in my garter and another in my handbag."

They entered the Lancia and it swung smoothly into the traffic. This time it was a sedan with a man and a girl close together on the front seat that took up the pursuit. Wentworth frowned as he lit a cigarette for Nita. That didn't look like a murder tail, but the mob might be lurking in the background, waiting for its chance to strike....

CHAPTER 8
THE SPIDER DRAWS BLOOD

T HE EVENING passed without any hostile attempt; and Wentworth had Nita leave separately and shift her hotel for safety's sake. He received a report from Ram Singh; but it was negative; Beatrice Ross, arrested as a material witness in the slaying, of Hackerson, was still a prisoner; her release not expected until the following, day. Wentworth rode home with the shadow on his trail, and he was still being followed next morning when he left his apartment.

He gave his shadow the slip and, in a subway wash-room, rapidly changed to the disguise he had assumed on the previous day, that of the blond young cavalry officer. He found Anse Collins waiting in the lobby of the hotel, standing on braced legs and scowling out of the window.

He nodded at Wentworth and strode, big-shouldered, across to meet him, but his scowl returned the moment they entered a taxi for the railway station. Wentworth eyed him curiously, but did not comment. Presently, watching behind them, he saw that once more they had a shadow. Whether the man he had dodged had succeeded in picking up the trail again, or whether they had kept watch on Collins also, Wentworth did not know. He was puzzled by the constant trailing and it was beginning to wear on his nerves. He wondered—at the purpose, but did not mention it to his companion.

Collins finally broke his silence gruffly as they alighted in front of the Pennsylvania Railway station, and strode along the wide corridor that led to the concourse. "What do you know about Briggs?" Collins growled.

The locomotive jumped the track, hurling
all the coaches over the embankment.

Wentworth looked at him quickly, told the man's position
and what his part was in the present case. Collins grunted. "He's
making a play for Nancy," he said, "and he's damned near old
enough to be her father."

Humor flickered in Wentworth's eyes, but he was careful not to let Collins see it. He had spotted their present shadow, a young woman, whose red hat was brave against the muggy day.

"Briggs took us to the hotel in his car last night," Collins grumbled. "Made a luncheon date with Nancy for today. He was tickled to death when I couldn't make it."

"Mrs. Collins is a very attractive woman," Wentworth said. "Going about a bit will help to take her mind off her troubles."

Collins lapsed into a sullen silence that lasted until they boarded the Middleton train. Wentworth saw that the girl in the red hat did not follow and he sat frowning out the window at the people hurrying up the platform, following red caps encumbered with suitcases and hatboxes. Unless the gangsters knew where Wentworth and Collins were going, there should be a shadow on the train now, yet he had spotted none. Collins was sitting hunched forward, elbows on his knees and hands clasped. "I guess Briggs is all right," he was saying grudgingly, "only… only…."

"Only you rather fancy Nancy yourself, eh?" Wentworth asked softly.

Collins colored. "Always was right fond of Nancy," he admitted slowly. "And I'm not aiming to have any damn Yankee—" he hesitated, eyeing Wentworth frankly. "I'm sorry, but that's the way I think of them. I ain't aiming to have anybody take advantage of her. And that Briggs is old enough to be her father."

Wentworth felt a slight impatience at the intrusion of this additional confusion into the situation. The whole story was plain enough. Anse Collins apparently had long planned to marry Nancy, but had given her up to his younger brother.

Now that his brother was dead, he didn't purpose to have any one else take her away from him.

A TOUCH of suspicion glanced across Wentworth's mind, but he thrust it aside instantly. Anse Collins would never be implicated in his brother's death, even though the action were inspired by so lovely a girl as Nancy Collins. The thought persisted that Anse Collins' misstep had been responsible for the mishap that had precipitated that first shooting scrape with Devil Hackerson, an affray that might well have proved fatal to the Spider. But Collins had been loyal enough since then. Nevertheless, Wentworth decided that he would find out where Collins had been at the time of his younger brother's death.

The train belched out of a tunnel into the open and the release of the close-crowded roar of the rails made the train seem wrapped in silence. The pale lights inside clicked out and Wentworth settled back in his seat with the air of a man who has traveled much and knows how to take his ease. His eyes were half-closed, but he was alertly watchful. Still the shadow did not evidence himself, and that fact nagged at the back of his mind. Why had they been followed to the train, then dropped?

Abruptly, Wentworth snapped erect in his seat. "Quick, Anse," he barked, "find the conductor and bring him forward."

Collins perked up his head, puzzled, then sprang to his feet. He was alert and quick-moving for a man of his size.

"What's the matter?" he demanded.

Wentworth did not wait to explain, but hastened forward

through the aisle followed by the curious stares of other passengers. To Wentworth there could be but one explanation of the failure of his shadow. A trail was no longer necessary, and that meant—danger! As he darted across steel platforms and into another coach, he flung a glance outside. They were ticking off an easy fifty miles an hour along the bank of the Hudson, the rails buttressed thirty or forty feet high with heaped-up jagged stones. A wreck at this point would kill scores and it would be a simple matter to apply some of the Master's chemical to the rails.

It would be like blowing up a mountain to chop down a tree, this wrecking a train to kill Wentworth. But the Master had not scrupled to knock over two skyscrapers and kill thousands for his own mysterious ends. Certainly he would not hesitate in this case. Another thought flashed through Wentworth's mind. This was an express train and undoubtedly would carry valuable mails. And it was evident the Master did not scorn to dig into other's pocketbooks with the help of his steel-eater.

A lurching jar threw Wentworth off his feet. He went flat down, catching himself on springing arms, then lay there as the jars continued. He did not have to see what was happening. He recognized those sounds, the concussions and lurching thump of the train. The locomotive had jumped the track and was bounding along out of control. It had dragged coaches off also. People were starting to their feet all over the car. A woman's voice rose shrilly and a baby wailed in fright.

WITH A violent sway and bump, a sickening twirl, the coach went over the embankment. The floor rose under Wentworth, pitched him against the seats on his right. He had a fragmentary glimpse through a window of jagged rock points racing toward them, then the window smashed and sent glass needles slashing through the air. A tearing jar. Wentworth clung to the side of the seat, felt his feet swing and knew that the coach had bounced and was rolling in the air. He hung on desperately.

His arms wrenched and the steel of the car clanged like a mightily struck anvil. His hands slipped from their hold. He curled his head down against his chest for protection, wrapped his arms about it and struck a cushioned back with his shoulders. He bounced, landed upon a man who grunted, then screamed, and suddenly realized that the roll of the car had ceased.

Drunkenly, he reeled to his feet, found he was standing on the ceiling of the car. Groans and frightened whimperings filled the car with a fearful symphony of pain. Off in another car, a man was screaming, over and over a single shrill note. The scream weakened and faded. Wentworth peered behind him, saw Anse Collins crumpled against a partition with a thread of blood across his temple. Beside him, the conductor pushed groggily to his feet, teetered for a moment on hands and feet and then straightened, struggling for balance.

Wentworth picked his way through broken glass and tumbled luggage to Collins' side, went hurriedly about reviving him. Abruptly, Wentworth snapped to his feet. He heard a faint sound as if some one were pounding an incredibly noisy typewriter with vehement finger. Through the intermittent chattering, a man shrieked. Collins came to with a jerk "A machine gun," he gasped.

"A hold-up," Wentworth snapped. "And the Master is behind it!"

He scrambled out through a broken window and raced along the embankment, a gun in each hand. The smashed cars were spilled over jumbled rocks, a sprawling, disjointed snake. Moans and screams punctuated the mechanical cackle of the gun. A group of men, carrying striped mail sacks over their shoulders, went down over the rocks with mountain-goat leaps.

Wentworth's guns blazed once, but he knew he was out of range. He charged on. It was impossible to advance in a straight line. He had to spring to right and left where flat surfaces offered secure footing, and that fact undoubtedly saved the Spider's life. A machine gun stammered from close at hand and powdered granite sprang up in dust directly in Wentworth's path. Only the fact that he had sprung sideways to better footing saved him. He jumped once more, going down on his knees between two chunks of granite. Lead buzzed past within inches of his head. He heard the deep boom of Collins' forty-four, but couldn't see the Southerner.

Cautiously, Wentworth squirmed between rocks down toward the spot where the machine gunner had hidden. He was cursing with impatience, knowing that the robbers were escaping, that it would be certain death to take up the pursuit before this machine gunner was eliminated. His trousers had been torn by that quick leap between the rocks. His scraped knees left a bloody trail. Collins' gun boomed again, and Wentworth jerked quickly into sight. He caught a glint of metal in a clump of bushes at the base of the embankment and sped ten shots in a continuous roll of fire from both guns.

Twigs flew high and the dead branches quivered and shook, then began to thrash violently. A man's hand slid into sight along the ground, gloved fingers clawing at the frozen ground. The hand and arm stiffened, then relaxed.

"Good work," Collins called, twenty feet to his right. "Man, that was good!"

WENTWORTH PEERED about. The robbers had vanished and over beyond a narrow strip of woods, automobile engines raced and dwindled into the distance. Wentworth's lips closed thinly. The bandits had escaped, but at least he had stopped one. He rock-leaped down the heap, hauled the man out of the bushes. At least six of Wentworth's bullets had hit him. Three had smashed through the side of his head.

Collins, pulling up just behind Wentworth, stared down and repeated: "Man, that *was* good!"

Wentworth scowled thoughtfully at the dead machine gunner. He knew that face. He was "Trigger" Skinner of Mickey McSwag's mob. Even as the Spider had guessed, his wiping out of Devil Hackerson had not hampered the Master in the least. He had had no trouble in finding other men who were willing to do his murdering for him to gain the secret of the chemical that turned vault doors into cake sugar.

Shoes rasping on rocks pulled Wentworth around and he saw two men running toward him with revolvers glinting in their fists. They were red-faced men, glowering beneath the pulled-down brims of felts. They eyed Wentworth suspiciously until they spotted "Trigger" Skinner dead on the ground, then admiration replaced the glare. "What'd you get him with, his own machine gun?" one growled.

Wentworth smiled grimly. "Automatic pistols are pretty deadly weapons, too, when properly used," he said drily. "Did they get away with anything?"

"Only ninety grand," snarled one of the men. "Not counting those the wreck killed, there's four dead men in the express car. We was riding passenger as an extra precaution or the typewriter would of caught us, too."

His remark confirmed Wentworth's surmise that the two were railroad detectives.

"Listen," he said. "I've got some damned important business to attend to in Middleton. Suppose it would be all right for me to shove along? It wouldn't make me sore if I didn't have to hang around to tell about this." A jerk of his head indicated the corpse of the gangster.

The detectives' eyes narrowed. They asked a few questions but in the end the men's hunger for praise won them over. They agreed to take credit for the kill. Wentworth pushed off up the rocky embankment toward where a relief train and autos had stopped, a half mile down the right of way. He and Collins could do no more good here.

Wentworth's face was white beneath the lean tan and his eyes smoldered as they surveyed the white-coated doctors climbing over the wreckage, the stretchers filing past toward the hospital car. Seven coaches were sprawled over the rocks, and the locomotive was a smashed wreck in the ravine. Two white splotches beside it, sheet-covered corpses, marked the resting place of the crew.

Wentworth's eyes rose to the glinting line of the steel rails, following it backward from the spot where the shattered engine lay. A few hundred feet back there was a break. His mouth lipless with compression, he walked rapidly to that spot and stared down at the crumbled wreckage of the rail. If there had been any doubt before that the Master was behind this carnage, a single glance at the track dissolved it. He stooped and picked up a segment of gray steel, struck it with another. There was no ring, only a sodden thud and fragments crumbled off and sifted gray powder on the ground.

CHAPTER 9
PREY OF THE MASTER

THE STEEL fell from his hands and as low bitter oath rasped his throat. He had counted thirty stretchers passing and men still labored to extract the injured and dead from the debris of the train. Was there no end to the infamy of this killer? Either Wentworth had accidentally taken the train which they intended looting, or the Master had deliberately wrecked it to get him at a disadvantage and mow him down. It looked suspiciously like that machine gunner had been planted solely to dispose of him—as if those shots had been fired partly to lure him from the protection of steel cars if he had survived the crash.

The Spider had killed the killer, but loot and slaughter had added to the villain's toll. This time there seemed more reason behind the atrocity that had been committed, but still the purpose behind the wrecking of the skyscrapers did not appear. The answer might be found in Middleton. Wentworth and Collins completed their trip to the town in relief automobiles, repaired their clothing—and went directly to the Collins apartment.

Collins stopped with an oath inside the door. The apartment was a wreck. Rugs had been stripped from the floor, pictures ripped from their moldings, overstuffed furniture cut to pieces. Drawers full of papers were tumbled upon the floor. Wentworth entered with a grimly satisfied smile. He made a telephone call, then from the wall above a closet door dug out a small camera and an electric fixture.

"Infra-red camera and light," he explained to Collins. "It could take a picture in darkness as well as light and the man it snapped would not be aware of the photograph. We'll have it developed."

Wentworth took the camera to a specialist shop and emerged to find extras being screamed in the streets. The headlines covered half the front page.

MUNICIPAL BUILDING CRASHES!
BANK LOOTED OF HALF MILLION!
GOVERNOR CALLS OUT TROOPS!

With hands as rigid as rock, and as cold, Wentworth gripped the paper to read the details. Truly, the Master had struck terribly in New York City. Apparently, he had only waited until Wentworth's back was turned to deal his most terrific blow. The death toll this time was only a thousand. The mockery of that qualifying word, "only," jeered at Wentworth like a grinning death's-head. But the casualties had been light as compared with the toll of the Sky and the Plymouth buildings.

The Municipal Building, which housed the "business offices of the city, had collapsed at the rush luncheon hour when the street was thronged with persons. Luckily, it had caved in upon itself, rather than plunging full length into jammed Park Row. If that had happened, the death toll might well have been several times as great. There had been no high wind, but engineers figured the constant jarring of subways beneath the building had broken down the crystallized steel.

Wentworth's burning eyes skipped from that account to the looting of the bank. It had occurred even as their train had been pulling out of Pennsylvania station. Machine guns had swept the entrance and interior of the bank clean of human life and steel shields had furnished no protection. They had crumpled like glass beneath the pounding bullets. The vaults had been no stronger and within minutes of the attack, the gangsters had rushed out with a fortune, the biggest robbery of its kind in history. Police were quickly on the scene and had managed to kill four of the robbers, but the rest had escaped.

A smaller item was the $250,000 robbery of an armored truck. Only the fact that a similar method had been used in this holdup even won it space on the front page. A large sedan had rolled up beside the armored truck and opened fire with machine guns. Under the hammer of the lead, the sides of the truck had crumpled. The guards had been literally riddled with bullets and the blood-stained loot snatched away. It had all happened within a space of moments. Three pedestrians had been burned down with the machine guns while they stood paralyzed by surprise.

AND NOW, martial law had been declared in New York City. Hereafter, bayonet-armed troops would patrol the street. A stringent curfew would be enforced, and no one could enter the financial district of the city where the banks were concentrated unless he had a special military permit. Wentworth saw the keen planning of Kirkpatrick behind these precautions, but he shook his head dubiously. Resources were being concentrated there under the supervision of the soldiers. Smaller banks, terrified by the ruthless efficiency of the attacks, were pouring their money into the strongly-protected centers. The insurance companies were responsible for that move, of course, insisting on these supposed safeguards under threat of vastly increased premiums. Couldn't the fools see that they were playing directly into the Master's hands?

Slowly, Wentworth folded the newspaper, looked up to find Collins white-faced and hot eyed. "I reckon Jim is better off dead," he said slowly. "If he knew that his invention was being used to kill people, he'd turn over in his grave."

With a wrench, Wentworth hurled the newspaper from him, stared about him at the throngs that were reading the extras. He saw men glance nervously over their shoulders at banks; he saw people move away from tall buildings with frightened strides. The panic was on. Until that monstrous Master was wiped out, men would walk in constant terror of their lives. Business was suffering already and once more the nation's faith in government and banks would reel. The industrial repercussions of this fright would send thunderous waves across the oceans and shake security there. A world that had buttressed its wealth behind steel—that protected its shores and borders with steel—would stare disintegration in the face.

"Listen," said Collins, "don't you reckon Alrecht might be behind this thing? You haven't even looked him up. I tell you, he and Bill Butterworth were the only folks that knew of Jim's invention."

Wentworth nodded shortly. "That's one of the reasons we came to Middleton today," he said. "You get to Butterworth and bring him down to our hotel room. I'll pay Mr. Alrecht a call. By that time, our infra-red film should be ready and we may know the answer to our problem."

Collins agreed, strode off with a long-legged determined pace, his face set and his heavy shoulders thrust forward. Wentworth watched him go with speculative eyes, then walked deliberately down Main Street toward the city's largest building, the First National Bank, in which Alrecht had law offices. As skyscrapers went, it wasn't very tall, but fourteen stories was an all-time high in Middleton. An elevator boy was arguing with the starter in the hall.

"I ain't hankering after being mashed in that cage," the boy said vehemently. "This is the tallest building in Middleton, and if those fellows come here, this will be the first place they hit. They're already robbed a bank here, and…."

"You can leave if you want to," the starter told him shortly, "but there isn't any need coming back tomorrow or the next day and expecting to get your job back."

The operator jeered, jerked off the coat that was the entire uniform and flung it on a chair. "This building ain't going to be here tomorrow," he said and strode toward the basement lockers. The starter crossed to the cage with an apologetic glance at Wentworth. "The whole town's half-crazy, sir," he said. "I'll take you up."

Wentworth caught himself listening for sounds in the building as the elevator rose, listening for creaking groans that might herald its collapse, and he cursed himself silently. Hell, he was getting as bad as that elevator boy. But his thoughts brought home with a shock to him how fearfully the terror of the steeleater was spreading. If the Spider, knowing more than anyone else about the gangsters—but he had to admit that his knowledge was terribly limited—could thus become nervous on merely entering a tall building, think of the effect of the spreading propaganda of fear upon the people as a whole!

ALRECHT'S OUTER office was well but not expensively furnished with brown leather chairs in a commodious waiting room. A girl clerk patted her metallic marcel as he told her that he was a police detective from New York City. She powdered her nose before she went into the inner office, but her calculating blue eyes were upon Wentworth again as she ushered him in. He walked with the slight swagger that unimportant men assume when, burdened with authority, they face a man who oversees them. He kept his hat on.

Alrecht was seated behind his desk, lounging back, toying

with a metal pencil with one hand. "What do you want?" he asked. There was no expression in his voice, either of hostility or welcome.

"Some dope about Jim Collins," Wentworth told him. He swaggered up to the desk and hooked his knee over a corner, leaned on it. "You was a pretty good friend of his, wasn't you?"

He studied the smallish man behind the desk. Alrecht was not old, though the wariness in his eyes was far from callow. Those eyes were watery, but had a strange quality of piercing regard. His hair lay neatly upon his large head, parted low on the side, and the parts had thinned peaks above his temples. His nose was sharp and aggressive, his mouth was secretive. There were little radiating lines along the upper lip that were prominent now as he pursed his mouth judiciously.

"Pretty good, yes," he agreed finally, with a nod. "But I knew his wife better than I knew him."

Wentworth leered. "Oh, that way, eh?" Alrecht's eyes lifted to his coldly and Wentworth straightened and took his knee off the desk. "No offense intended, counselor," he said quickly.

"I hope not," Alrecht replied gently.

Wentworth was acting out his role of detective to perfection, but behind the mask of crudity and swagger authority, he was keenly estimating this man. Alrecht was shrewd, beyond any doubt, and nervousness was evident in the slow, studied movements of his hands. He was fighting a tendency to fidget with that metal pencil. He slapped it down abruptly, and clasped his hands together. The fingers closed tightly.

97

"Come to the point," he said sharply. "I have no time to idle away like this."

"Of course not, of course not," Wentworth agreed. "The commissioner wanted to know if you had any idea what this invention of Jim Collins' was. Miz' Collins, she says you was to finance it if it went over."

Alrecht shook his head. "No, I didn't know what it was. Jim was very secretive about it. All he said was it would make us all rich if I'd help him. And of course I was glad to do that—for Mrs. Collins' sake."

"I see," Wentworth nodded sagely. "Know Bill Butterworth?" Was he mistaken, or had Alrecht started at that sudden mention of the chemist who worked with Collins?

"I've met him," Alrecht said cautiously, after a perceptible pause. "He was another chemist at the place where Jim worked. In fact I had dinner with him last night, trying to find if he knew anything of Jim's processes—for Mrs. Collins' sake, of course."

"Of course," Wentworth agreed, and he masked his sarcasm so lightly that Alrecht looked at him sharply for a long moment before he went on talking.

"Butterworth said he didn't know anything about it, but he seemed to be more prosperous than I ever remember seeing him before." Alrecht paused as if weighing his words. "He had on a new suit and he seemed mightily pleased with himself. Told me he'd had an extra allowance from home and was planning to run back and surprise the folks. He was English, you know. I tried to get hold of him at the plant today and he had left. They said he had resigned."

Wentworth frowned heavily. "That looks mighty suspicious."

Alrecht nodded slowly, and there was a gleam back of his pale, queerly keen eyes. "I thought so, and here's something else. Night before last I was driving through the Outerdale section—that's where the Collins lived you know—and I'll swear I saw Butterworth *sneaking* along the street. Sneaking, mind you! I started to stop him, but he clearly didn't want to be recognized so I thought better of it."

ALRECHT SPREAD his hands, palm upward. Wentworth saw that they were moist. "I don't want to make trouble for Butterworth, but it all seems damnably suspicious. And I'll tell you something else. It's just a hunch, you understand, but I believe it's a good one. I believe that Jim's invention is being used by these men who robbed the bank here!"

"No!" Wentworth cried.

Alrecht nodded solemnly.

"Jeez!" said Wentworth. "There might be something in that at that. Jim Collins was a steel chemist... *say!* I'm going to find this Bill Butterworth."

He started toward the door. "Thanks a lot, Mr. Alrecht."

Alrecht jerked his chin up, lowering his eyes, a gesture to wait. "Just a minute, my man," he said. He got deliberately to his feet and circled the desk. He put a hand on Wentworth's arm and looked seriously into his eyes. "I'd much rather my name wasn't mentioned in connection with this," he said. "Tell your superiors if you have to, but..." He smiled patronizingly, tapped Wentworth on the shoulder. "Why not turn the idea in as your own?"

"You wouldn't mind?" Wentworth registered suppressed eagerness.

"Not at all."

"Thanks, Mr. Alrecht, I won't forget this," Wentworth said feelingly, and walked out. Once in the hall, his forehead creased in a frown. Just what, he wondered, was Alrecht's game? It was obvious that he was trying to throw suspicion on Butterworth, and it was just as obvious that he knew much more about the invention than he was willing to tell.

Furthermore, Wentworth was not entirely sure that he had put over the imposture perfectly. There had been one or two occasions when suspicion had gleamed in Alrecht's queer eyes. He had been inclined to discount Anse Collins' ideas about Alrecht, laying them down to his obvious jealously over Nancy. Now, he was not sure. Alrecht scarcely seemed the egocentric killer that the Master was, yet the man certainly had an essential conceit.

Collins was waiting for Wentworth at the hotel. "Butterworth has skipped town," he growled. "Hasn't been seen since he left his boarding house last night. All his clothes had been cleaned out some time back, and he owes a wad of bills around town."

Wentworth responded with only a slight nod. His mind was still occupied with the puzzle about Alrecht. To his way of thinking, Butterworth's departure was simply fortuitous for the lawyer. But why had he mentioned seeing Butterworth near the Collins apartment? With a sudden oath, Wentworth wheeled and started for the door.

"Get that picture from the camera shop and come to Alrecht's office with it fast," he snapped.

Collins' quick query was cut off by the slamming door and Wentworth went downstairs in great striding bounds, ignoring the elevator. He was furious with himself. Why hadn't he seen the significance of that story about Butterworth when he was in the lawyer's office? It was obvious enough that the man had been trying to throw suspicion on the chemist and had mentioned his supposed sight of him near the Collins home *because Alrecht knew the home had been searched!*

Only guilty knowledge of the searching could have inspired Alrecht's lie about Butterworth and that confiding eager rush of information. Either Alrecht had performed that search himself or he had paid some one to do it. His talkativeness alone was enough to cause suspicion. Long strides hurled Wentworth across the lobby, into a taxi at the curb.

"First National Building fast," he snapped.

They got there fast, but it wasn't fast enough. When he reached Alrecht's office, the lawyer had gone. The girl with the metallic hair tossed her head at him and delicately powdered her nose. "Mr. Alrecht has gone to New York," she said. "He was called into consultation on an important case."

She slapped her hand down on the desk, whirled her chair as Wentworth stalked past her toward the door of the inner office.

"You can't do that," she protested.

THE INNER office was empty. Wentworth crossed to a telephone. The girl came across and put both hands on the other side of the desk. Her arms were stiff. "Say, what do you think this is?" she demanded.

"Long distance," said Wentworth into the transmitter. "Long distance? Mr. Alrecht calling. I wanted to verify a long distance call that came through your office for me within the last fifteen minutes. It has occurred to me that some friends of mine might be playing a joke… Yes, thank you very much."

Alrecht had been called to New York, and by a firm of prominent attorneys. The long distance operator confirmed the phone message.

Wentworth frowned and left the shrill girl talking loudly with her hands planted on her hips. Collins almost smacked into him in the hall.

"Say, that guy can't develop the film. Says he ain't got something or other he needs. I took the film away from him." He thrust a wrapped package into Wentworth's hands.

"Hell, the breaks are certainly against us!" Wentworth said impatiently as they went to the elevator. He had counted on that film and now it couldn't be developed until he reached New York. But they could reach New York soon after Alrecht, overtake him at the lawyers' offices. There would be no trains for hours because of the wreck, but an automobile would take them to the city quickly. They left the building hurriedly and climbed into a taxi. It started a leisurely trundle down Main street. Suddenly the taxi driver squealed and yanked on his wheel. His motor roared and sent the cab reeling down a side street. Wentworth flung forward, set a hand on the man's collar.

"What the hell…?" he began. Then his voice was smashed

into fragments. Rumbling thunderous concussion swept over and past him. The taxi bumped over the curb, side-swayed and rammed its nose against a brick wall, stopped with a jarring crash that sent the windshield back in the driver's lap. He sat motionless, his shoulders rising in little jerks with his heavy breathing.

"Jeez!" he panted out. *"Jeez!"*

Wentworth was out of the taxi now and pelting back toward Main street.

He saw a dark huddle in the middle of the street, a huddle from which slow thick lines of crimson crawled their way. It was half of a woman's body. The other half was in a hole in the street beneath a building block. Around the corner, Wentworth whirled and stopped dead. The First National Bank building was a jumble of broken masonry and shattered steel scattered along Main street. A streetcar had been passing and its battered walls leaned crazily above its steel trucks, but it had no top and no bottom. Within it, no one even moaned.

It came to Wentworth's consciousness presently that a heavy hand was biting into his arm. He turned to see Collins, white-faced, at his elbow.

"God," Collins gulped, "and you were complaining about the breaks. If we hadn't been in a big hurry getting away from there…!"

Wentworth said nothing. He was thinking of that noisy little blond stenographer, a pert little thing with her powder puff and her metallic hair. Somewhere in that mess, they would find her body—if anything was left of it. He turned about, feeling suddenly sick and walked heavily down the sidewalk.

Feet slapped the pavement hurriedly behind him, but he didn't turn, saw no reason to turn until a hard prod of iron jabbed into his back.

"Hands up, you two," a breathless voice ordered. "I saw you two run out of that there bank a minute afore she caved in."

Wentworth turned, looked into a policeman's flushed face. "Don't be silly," he said. "I had business with Mr. Alrecht. You can ask..." He paused suddenly, realizing the utter futility of that phrase. Poor little noisy kid, crushed somewhere in that pile. The stenographer couldn't testify to anything.

"You can't fool me," the officer said angrily. "I saw you run out of there, and you're coming along to headquarters...."

Wentworth was suddenly conscious of a growing crowd about them. Of tense, angry faces thick behind the officer, of mutters and clenched fists.

"What is it?" one man asked another.

"The cop caught the two guys that pushed over the First National...."

"Don't be a fool," Collins snapped. He pushed toward the officer. "I'm a deputy sheriff and we had just been to see a lawyer in that building."

"Get back! Get back!" the officer yelled wildly. He backed up, waving his revolver. "Here, you men. Help me."

The mutter became an angry shouting, then a roar. There were fifty persons crowded about the tableau of Wentworth and Collins and the officer. They closed in with a rush.

"Lynch them!" a voice yelled out, somewhere back in the crowd. "They killed more than a hundred people!"

CHAPTER 10
BRIGGS' CONFESSION

WENTWORTH THREW both hands high above his head as men jostled him and hands snatched savagely at his clothing.

"Officer, I demand that you protect me," he snapped. "You got us into this, now get us out of it!"

The policeman was white-faced, frightened at the sudden violence of the mob. He lifted his gun up above his head and squeezed the trigger twice.

"Stop it!" he shouted. "There ain't going to be no lynching!"

Somebody snatched the gun out of his hand; somebody else brought a stone down on the policeman's head. Wentworth wrenched free of the men about him, leaped forward. He saw a man level the gun and kicked out viciously. His shoe cracked against the weapon, spun it high into the air. The man moaned and doubled over a broken wrist.

Wentworth lifted the policeman, hands beneath his arms. Through a tangle of threatening fists, he spotted Collins. The tall Southerner was standing on braced feet, his fists were striking with beautifully timed precision. A man caught an uppercut and stiffened, his back arching as he pitched backward. He took two others with him. Collins' arm drew back fast, the elbow flying out behind him. It caught a man's belly and he doubled over, groaning.

That cleared a ring immediately around Collins and his quick glance sought Wentworth. There was a fighting gleam in his brown eyes, a small hard smile on his mouth.

"Give me a hand with this cop, Collins," Wentworth called. "Somebody hurt him."

Collins put out his two arms breast-stroke fashion and opened a way through the ranks. Men fell away from in front of him.

"Get an ambulance for the cop," Wentworth called. "Somebody slugged him. There's going to be trouble about this."

Collins caught hold of the cop's feet with one hand and hit about him with his right. "Get out of the way," he said angrily. "Can't you see the man's hurt?"

The crowd was in confusion now. Few had been close enough around the policeman to know which had been the accused men. A number of those had been knocked out, and others had fled in fright when the policeman was attacked. The crowd gave way before Collins' angry shouts and the two carried the cop into a drugstore.

"We'll bring in some more of the injured," Wentworth told the clerk. "See what you can do for this poor fellow."

He caught Collins by the arm and pulled him out. The crowd parted at the doorway.

"You better make yourself scarce," Wentworth said, looking several in turn straight in the eye. "That cop is going to be madder than hell when he finds his gun gone and knows that somebody slugged him."

He pushed through the crowd, Collins behind him and they hurried down the street. An excited boy followed them for three blocks, pointing at them and saying they had killed a policeman, but they lost him finally in the rush of people to the scene of the disaster.

"We've got to get back to New York quickly," Wentworth told Collins. "I don't know whether the collapse of that building back there was aimed at us or not, but it damned near caught us. And this camera contains valuable evidence. I'm sure of that. It may even have a picture of the Master himself. You go directly to those lawyers' offices as soon as we hit the city. Get on Alrecht's tail and don't lose him. I think I'll have a warrant for his arrest pretty soon after we get there."

Collins said quietly, "I won't lose him, Spider."

Wentworth hired a car and shoved the accelerator to the floor as they swept out of the end of Main Street onto the highway. The rush of air, the drone of the motor drowned all other sounds. The cold bite of the wind was like a knife through Wentworth's temples, sent his blood racing through his body, stimulated his brain.

HE KNEW that as soon as the policeman regained consciousness, he would give detailed descriptions of himself and Collins to the state's wide police broadcast. They would be named as suspects in all the fearful tragedies that had paralyzed the world in recent days—Wentworth realized with a shock that it had been only forty-eight hours since collapse of the Sky Building had heralded this era of terror.

With brief words, tossed out the corner of his mouth, he told Collins what threatened. "This car will be identified right off," he said, "for those police can move fast when anything as important as this is involved. We would better separate. You take my coat and hat. I'll alter your eyebrows and put a mustache on you. I'll shed my clothes and make a few other changes, then we'll drop this car."

He whirled it off the road into a lane between trees. The narrow way dipped sharply and they were soon hidden from the highway. He made the changes in Collins' appearance swiftly, sent him on the way in the car.

"Junk it in the first town," he ordered. "Hire a taxi to take you to New York. Got money?"

"I reckon I can make out all right," Collins drawled. There was excitement behind his voice. "This is the first time, though, I ever run away from a fight."

Wentworth laughed brittlely. "You'll get your full dose of fighting before this is over, fellow," he said. "We're closing in on the Master. He's trying too hard to kill us for me to think anything else. And another thing—I don't fight the police."

"I'd noticed," Collins said dryly.

Wentworth finished his work on Collins, eyed him a second and nodded. "You'll do," he said, "but if I were you I'd put a pebble in one of your shoes. That will make you limp and change the way you carry yourself."

Collins' eyes were still amused. "I reckon you're pretty good,

Spider," he said, stooping to thrust a pebble into his shoe. He got in the car. "If they spot this boat, they're going to have a swell chase before they catch me."

The engine roared in reverse; the car bounced rapidly about and spurted up the hill with gravel flying from under the tires. Wentworth watched it out of sight, then stripped off mustache and wig, shrugged his shoulders into Collins' coat. It was a bit loose, but not conspicuously so. He had spotted a farmhouse a half mile back from the road and he made his way toward it. He traveled at a pace that would have been impossible for a man inexperienced in woodcraft.

The windows of the house on the hill were boarded tight. Apparently it was a summer residence. There was a two-story garage back of it and an open-faced shed strung out behind that. In front of the shed was an old Buick truck, resting on flat tires. Wentworth smiled cheerfully and went to work. There was a five-gallon gasoline-can in the garage and it was half full. A pump got some air into the tires. There was almost no life in the battery, but by dint of much sweating and pushing, he got the truck to the head of a long hill and started it down. It back-fired twice after a fifty-yard roll. Twenty-five more yards and it caught and died. At the foot of the hill, it spluttered and died again. Wentworth spun the loosened motor with a crank and finally it rattled noisily to life.

THE NEXT town was almost fifteen miles away and it took Wentworth an hour to make it in the truck. He left the truck on the street and had no trouble hiring a car to take him to New York. In the city, he drove through the early dusk directly to

Kirkpatrick's office, gave him the infra-red camera with information as to where it had been installed and asked that he set technicians to work at once to develop it. Beatrice Ross was still a prisoner, but her lawyer had begun a *habeas corpus* fight and might free her at any time. Wentworth left the room to phone that information to Ram Singh and warn the Hindu once more of the importance of trailing the woman and Baldy. Then he called Nita, had her return to her apartment and pack clothing for a trip which he did not explain.

The commissioner's face had grown haggard and lined with fatigue, and despite his meticulous dress, he had an impressed look about him.

"These disasters are fearful, Dick," he said heavily. "And it's one case I can't crack at all. I can't understand the motive behind it. The train wreck and the bank and armored car holdups are simple enough, but why the destruction of those buildings?"

"I still have no clue to that," Wentworth admitted, "but I have found some suspicious circumstances." And he told him about Alrecht and the man's sudden, but apparently explicable departure for New York City—the fact that Collins was trailing him. "When we get that photograph developed," Wentworth said, "I think we may have something that will make Alrecht talk. Even if he is not the Master, I think he has guilty knowledge."

The door opened and Nancy Collins walked in. There was a flush to her cheeks and her eyes were bright. Behind her, Briggs, the consultant architect, came short-legged into the room. His movements were quick as always, but there was a heaviness about him.

"Mr. Briggs has something to tell you, Mr. Kirkpatrick," Nancy said.

She nodded to Wentworth, remembering his name from their previous introduction in the commissioner's office. It was apparent that Briggs was acutely miserable. He had the butt of a cold cigar clamped between his teeth and his long hair was rumpled. He laid a soft black felt hat on the desk.

"Damned fool," Briggs muttered and glanced up, half sheepishly at Kirkpatrick. "Only one excuse," he went on in his queer staccato speech. "My daughter. I'm damn' fond of Betty."

Kirkpatrick was frowning. "What the hell are you talking about, Briggs?"

Briggs looked up at Nancy Collins under his brows, then seemed to shrug off his lethargy. "Mrs. Collins made me talk," he said. He took the cigar out of his mouth, jabbed its wet end at Kirkpatrick. "There is a way to stop this business of buildings collapsing."

"*What?*" Kirkpatrick snapped forward, hands hard on the desk. He was abruptly red with anger, cords swelled in his throat. "A way to stop it! You knew and didn't tell us?" He came around the desk fast, caught Briggs by the collar and jerked the little man almost off his feet. "What the hell do you mean?"

Wentworth had never seen Kirkpatrick so angry, he thought, as he stepped calmly forward, touched his friend on the shoulder.

"Let's hear what he's got to say, Kirk," he urged quietly.

Kirkpatrick whipped his head about, eyes flashing, then visibly fought down his anger. He took his hand off Briggs' collar, stepped back a half-pace although his eyes still glared.

"Out with it!" he ordered.

"Not sure of it," Briggs muttered. "Don't blame you for being that way. Feel that way myself. But, Mr. Kirkpatrick," he drew himself up to his full short height, met the commissioner's glare directly. "They kidnapped my daughter—kidnapped Betty. Told me that if I told, they'd send her back—*little piece at a time!*" HIS FACE was twisted. "But Nancy—Mrs. Collins—made me talk. After today and all those others that have been killed."

"The process, man!" Kirkpatrick roared. "What will stop the steel-eater?"

Briggs shook his head. "It isn't that," he said. "It's a different steel. Steel-eater won't hurt it. My belief it won't. Bessmo process stuff. They claim it won't crystallize. From what analysis shows, this steel-eater won't hurt it."

Kirkpatrick frowned. He shook his head. "That would mean bracing all the buildings, replacing girders, everything with this different type of steel?" he asked slowly.

"Practically that," Briggs nodded. "You see, it isn't really feasible." The man was pleading for forgiveness for not having spoken before. Nancy Collins' eyes were bright upon him. He looked sidewise at her again, back to Kirkpatrick. "For God's sake," he said suddenly, hoarsely. "Let somebody else make the discovery. My Betty… All I've got in the world…."

He turned and stumbled blindly and Wentworth shoved a chair in his path. He gripped its back and stood breathing heavily. Kirkpatrick was staring down at the floor. "It's worth trying," he said finally. "Dick, would Professor Brownlee stand for the announcement coming from him?"

"Probably," Wentworth said. "If he believed it was true."

"We'll find out," Kirkpatrick said grimly. He spun to the telephone, began barking orders. The president of the Bessmo concern was to be located and hailed to New York. Wentworth stood in the background and a light flamed in his eyes. When Kirkpatrick paused for a moment, he asked quietly if there was a directory of directors of corporations in the place. Kirkpatrick nodded impatiently and Wentworth strode, eager-eyed, from the office. He found the book, ran over the list of stockholders in the Bessmo. One of them was Alrecht.

A man wearing thick-lensed glasses, his blond hair rumpled, hurried into the outer office with a strip of wet paper in his hands. He headed straight for Kirkpatrick's office, went in after a brief knock. Wentworth strode after him, saw the man lay the paper on Kirkpatrick's desk.

"Here's the film from the infra-red camera, sir," the man said, speaking in a high, flustered voice. "It's not perfect, sir, but with the short time allowed me...."

Wentworth spun past him and gazed down at the strip of paper. The photograph, all intense blacks and whites with no group, showed a masked man standing in the middle of a disordered room. He had a long pair of scissors in one hand and was peering about him. His lips were pursed and worried. Wentworth laughed shortly.

"Kirk, the case seems to be solved," he said excitedly. "The motive for the destruction of the buildings was the popularization of Bessmo steel. On the list of directors, the big stock-holders, is that man there." He pointed at the masked man in the photograph. *"Alrecht!"*

CHAPTER 11
A DANGEROUS GAME

KIRKPATRICK SNATCHED his phone, ordered Alrecht's immediate arrest, but he was frowning as he leaned back in his chair, staring doubtfully at the photograph.

"But, damn it, man," he said. "If they wanted to popularize Bessmo steel, why kidnap Briggs' daughter and hold her as a price for Briggs' silence?"

"To avert suspicion," Wentworth said swiftly. "The steel must be well enough known for the truth to come out sooner or later. They must have known that Briggs would talk after a while and that the story of his daughter's kidnapping would come out. That would still leave us in the dark as to the motive behind the entire case."

Kirkpatrick shook his head. "I'm not satisfied," he said.

Wentworth grinned. "I'm not, either," he admitted. "But I still think that Alrecht can give us some interesting information about the case. I suggest that we check all the stockholders of that Bessmo company at once, check on the lives of the men...."

"But," Briggs came forward timidly, but doggedly. "My daughter, Betty, what about her?"

"We'll find her," Kirkpatrick said emphatically. "Got a picture?"

Briggs fumbled in his pocket, brought out a Kodak picture. "Men who stole her tore up every picture in the house," he said painfully. "Mrs. Collins found this one. Old album."

Kirkpatrick took the picture. It showed a smallish girl with a merry Irish face. She had on a man's hat, a large one and she was gripping it with both hands, pulling it down over her ears. It was sizes too big for her.

"We took that one day on a picnic," Briggs said. "Always made fun of my long hair. Big hats…" He struck a match and lit the cold stump between his teeth. His hand trembled and he puffed furiously at the cigar, sent out billows of smoke.

"Tell me about your daughter's kidnapping," Kirkpatrick said. He spoke gruffly. He was not unsympathetic with Briggs. As the little man said, the truth about Bessmo was important, but its peculiar power to resist crystallization was not of overwhelming immediate value. In time it might protect the people. It might be used to brace buildings against future attacks of the steel-eater, but the information was useless in the present crisis.

The story of the kidnapping was soon told. Betty was a madcap girl with a bright temper, and on a certain evening she had quarreled with her escort while at a friend's home she had coolly taken his car and driven away, returning to her own home alone. Apparently the kidnappers had been waiting for some time for an opportunity to strike. This had been the occasion. They had seized her, used her keys to enter the house and destroy the pictures—apparently to hinder police in any possible search—then carried her away. Once every day she was permitted to talk to Briggs over the phone, a set formula: "Hello, daddums, I'm all okay."

Then the wire would close. Briggs had insisted on this proof that his daughter was alive before he would yield to the kidnapper's demands. "I don't know what will happen now," he said miserably. "I tried to ransom her, but they only laughed at me. I'm not a rich man, you know."

He looked up with his bright little eyes through the veil of vile-smelling cigar smoke. "Going home now," he said simply. "Betty's due to call in any hour."

"Did anyone see the kidnappers enter the house?" Wentworth asked quietly.

"No," Briggs said, "but one of the hall-boys of our apartment saw a man. Hung around the two days before they got her. Man with bald head. Cast in one eye."

WENTWORTH STRAIGHTENED with sucked-in breath. Kirkpatrick looked at him and they nodded. Baldy had shown up again. Everywhere they turned in their quest for the men behind the steel-eater, for the Master, they ran across this man with no criminal past, this bald man with a head like a dome and a cast in one eye. The entire case seemed to devolve on finding him.

"If you don't mind, Kirk," said Wentworth, rising, "I'd like to work on this kidnapping case."

Kirkpatrick studied him speculatively with fatigued eyes. To him, it seemed distinctly a side-issue to the main case: the snaring of the Master, the capture of Alrecht and the questioning of big stockholders in Bessmo. He shrugged.

"If you wish to, Dick," he agreed. "Of course, we'll attempt to trace the call from the girl when it comes through. You'll get in touch with Professor Brownlee right away?"

Wentworth nodded. "As soon as we find that the steel actually will do what it's supposed to. Personally, I think there is no doubt about it."

Kirkpatrick continued to eye him, then they shook hands and Wentworth left with Briggs and Nancy Collins. The architect was morose and silent throughout the drive to his Riverside Drive apartment and his cigar went out between his teeth. They dropped Nancy at her hotel and pushed on. Wentworth leaned back in a corner and stared out at the night scene with half-closed eyes. It was splitting small hard snow and the flying specks whipped upward across the windshield and danced in little eddies on the pavement of the street. Each time they passed a corner, the smash of the gust from the river would sway the car.

In the nineties, Briggs spun the car downhill into the teeth of that wind, parked on the side street and fought his door open against a half-gale. They ducked across the walk into the protection of the apartment-house doorway, stamped their feet and blew on their fingers as they went along a tiled hallway to the elevators. The Negro operator got up from a chair in a corner and crossed to the cages.

Briggs pushed open the door of his apartment and walked along a long hall. He went directly to a davenport in a corner where a telephone stood on a stand at his elbow. Hard grains of snow made a gusty whispering against the windows behind him and moaned around the corners of the house.

Briggs had a fresh cigar between his teeth and that had gone out also. The phone tinkled and he snatched it from its cradle before the first bell note had been completed. He held it to his ear, hesitated, staring straight ahead of him, then got out a husky, "Hello!"

His eyes brightened and he said, "I'm glad, darling. Can't you…?" He choked off, put the phone slowly back on its cradle. He looked up dully at Wentworth.

"She's all right," he said.

Wentworth questioned Briggs briskly about the disappearance of his daughter, touching several new angles that had occurred to him since leaving Kirkpatrick's office, but he elicited nothing new and left soon afterward. George took a brown whistle from a nail near the elevator shaft, whistled loudly for a cab from the doorway, but none came and Wentworth thanked him, and holding his hat, ducked out into the wind. It pushed him up the hill and he turned to the right, hugging the wall for the comparative warmth of its protection. There was a delicatessen store at the corner which had a telephone-booth, and from it he called Kirkpatrick, then Jackson at his apartment, then Nita. He was on the point of calling a cab when he recalled that there was a Drive-it-Yourself stand just around the corner toward the underpass that ducked beneath Riverside Drive. He went there and arranged for a closed car, for he expected to do much traveling tonight, and his own car probably would be dangerous, and cabs were busy.

HIS CALL to police headquarters had elicited the information that Beatrice Ross was about to be released, that

Betty Briggs had phoned from a drug store in Brooklyn, but a check-up there had failed to reveal any girl having been in the booth. The drug clerk was positive of that because he had had only four or five customers the entire evening and none had been women.

Wentworth puzzled over that information as he drove through the storm toward Nita's apartment in the Riverside Towers. It tied up in one way. Mickey McSwag's mob was strong in Brooklyn and McSwag was apparently the gangster the Master was using now. Nita greeted him at the door and shivered when he clasped her warm hands in his.

"You must be almost frozen," she told him. "I've got hot coffee and some of that Courvoisier '98 you like so well."

With a bound and a cavernous bark, a big Harlequin Great Dane sprang past Nita and reared with its paws on Wentworth's shoulders, huge head high above his own, tongue lolling in greeting. Wentworth thumped his fist against the dog's chest and laughed.

"Down, Apollo," he ordered and threw an arm about Nita's waist as they strolled back along the hall into her studio apartment. "Apollo can't get used to being grown up," he said. "If he starts romping, the people below you are apt to have plaster in their faces."

The Great Dane that Wentworth had trained from puppyhood after importing him for Nita stalked along beside him as they entered the studio living-room. The big windows that opened on the river were covered by the warm folds of crimson velvet curtains and on a stone hearth, a fire leaped and blazed.

Coffee steamed in an electric urn on a small table, and there was a slim-necked bottle of cognac beside it.

But Wentworth did not drop into the chair placed invitingly beside it. He strode energetically up and down the room, tossed his overcoat and hat into a chair. He flexed his fingers, chaffed them rapidly together.

"We're near the break," he told her. "I'm going out to find Briggs' daughter tonight." He spun the story of her kidnapping. "When I locate her, I'll be close to this Baldy who's running things for the Master. Once I get to Baldy...."

Nita laughed. "It doesn't sound like you're very close to the Master, Dick." He grinned, rumpled her bronze curls with his hands and kissed her when she protested. "It's you, darling, that makes me enthusiastic. Just being here for the little while I can stay makes a new man out of me." He caught Nita by the hands and pulled her to her feet, clasped her close into his arms. For a long minute they stood like that while the fire crackled and popped and threw their merged shadow in giant size across the ceiling. Then Wentworth released her. They were serious-eyed now as they looked at each other.

The service-door opened quietly and Ram Singh appeared after a moment, bowing from the arch that led to the breakfast room. Wentworth, his eyes still on Nita, drew in a deep breath. Abruptly he drove somberness from his face with a cheerful grin that touched, but did not entirely brighten his eyes. He spun to Ram Singh and spluttered out staccato Hindustani.

Ram Singh, answering, said that Jackson had replaced him just as Beatrice Ross had been released. There was a somber protest in his words at being pulled off of such an important mission. Wentworth told him, smiling, knowing the rivalry of service between Jackson and Ram Singh, that he had a task which only the Hindu could do.

The Hindu bowed again, touching his cupped hands to his forehead in a deep *salaam*. His eyes were proud now. Wordlessly, he backed into the half-darkness and returned a moment later with a small black suitcase. He set it upon a table and opened it as Wentworth dropped into a chair. Ram Singh whipped out a towel and tucked it beneath his master's chin, went swiftly to work upon his face with make-up tools.

AS RAM SINGH worked, Wentworth talked to Nita in snatches. "We've succeeded in tracing Butterworth up to a certain point," he said. "He got a passport and had it viséed for Great Britain. He has relatives in Kent. I want you and Ram Singh to catch the *Berengaria*, sailing at midnight and trace him down. I'll have passports made out for you by radio. Butterworth must come back, or you must get the story from him about Collins' invention and about everyone who knows anything about it."

"Then you aren't so near to the break of the case?" asked Nita quietly.

A hint of a smile twitched Wentworth's lips. "I'm always just around the corner," he said, "but like prosperity, it may be a long, slow corner to turn. If my present plans fail, there must be another move already in preparation."

"You're quite sure, Dick," Nita asked slowly, "that you don't simply want me out of the country for safety? You haven't let me do much on this case."

"I'll be glad to have you safe," Wentworth told her gravely, "but there is much more than that. Your work may in many respects be the turning point of the whole case. I don't dare entrust what information you may gain to anyone else. It seems quite clear that Butterworth is dodging someone, possible police. He left many unpaid debts behind in Middleton. We have been unable to find what ship he took abroad. That's why I'm sending Ram Singh with you. It may come to physical battle before you get what you want from him. At the same time, I think that it can be handled better without police help."

Ram Singh fitted a covering like a wig over Wentworth's head and Nita uttered a startled exclamation. "You're posing as Baldy!" she cried.

Wentworth lifted a small hand mirror and peered at the result of the covering. Fitted rightly over his head was a bald dome that glistened like an egg. He nodded, grinning slightly.

"A good job, Ram Singh," he said softly. "Some days ago," he told Nita, "I anticipated that the need for this imposture might occur and had Ram Singh prepare the disguise."

He stopped talking, tilted his head back while Ram Singh dropped liquid into his eyes, lifted the lids and fitted bits of concave glass under them against the eyeballs. He closed his eyes, turned toward Nita and opened them. The piercing blue-gray gaze of the Spider had vanished. The left eye was a pale blue and there was a cast in it. The right eye was dull and brown.

"Those Zeiss lenses," said Nita softly.

Wentworth nodded. "They're a bit uncomfortable for a while, but I've become, quite accustomed to them. It's not very easy to see with the colors painted on them, but we've perfected a film paint that permits me to see through fairly well. And in the middle of each, there's a small hole for the pupil."

He stood up, stepped into a dressing room to one side and shortly emerged with a greasy cap pulled down over his dome head. His shoulder sloped beneath an old gray overcoat that was too short for him and he walked with a furtive shuffle that took inches off his height.

"I've never seen Baldy," Wentworth said, "but Ram Singh has and he has a remarkable memory for such detail."

He tried a number of voice tones under Ram Singh's coaching and soon had acquired a squeaky, changeable voice that caused the Hindu's turbaned head to nod in satisfaction, Wentworth balled the overcoat and cap into the suitcase, donned his own and pulled his felt well down upon his head. He bowed over Nita's hands, raising them to his lips.

"I may see you on the *Berengaria,*" he told her. "If not, I'll phone you tomorrow. You have two hours before sailing. You'll find your passage reserved. Jenkyns attended to that." He straightened and Nita came close to him, raised her lips.

She shuddered slightly. "I don't really feel it's you, Dick, behind that disguise," she complained, then laughed and kissed him again. Her arms tightened about his shoulders convulsively. "Be careful, Dick," she whispered against his mouth.

CHAPTER 12
THE GAME IS LOST

RECALLING NITA'S warning three quarters of an hour later as he swung right off Manhattan Bridge, Wentworth's disguised lips twitched slightly. The rush and beat of the wind rocked the little coupé as he pushed it southward along the water front through the whip of the snow. In a few blocks now, he would be on the edge of what had been McSwag's "territory" during the great era of the rackets. That was finished now, but McSwag had turned to other criminal revenue. His mob of gunmen was the most ruthless and deadly in this post-repeal period. They robbed and killed and their immunity of prohibition days was still a shield and buckler for them.

The Master had done well to choose them—if he had a strong hand. Otherwise, McSwag might well take him over and make him serve his own ends. Wentworth would need to be more than careful to play the game he planned tonight and come out with his life. He would have to be bold and swift. His keen mind must not fail him for a second.

He gassed around a corner into Water Street. Out of the side window, he could see the far end of Brooklyn Bridge, hazed by snow, the swoop of its cables picked out by dim lights. He would be directly under it in another block. Two blocks beyond that was the pool-room-saloon where McSwag's mob usually hung out. Wentworth held down his impatience and let the coupé jounce along over the cobbles, at a slow speed. There was no reason for Baldy to hurry, how ever much the Spider might yearn to join battle.

The neon-light sign before the restaurant spilled a bloody trail across the sidewalk, sent a crimson glow out against the haze of falling snow. Wentworth spun the coupé around in a U curve and parked on the edge of that glow, eased out and shuffled to the doors, his shoulders hunched against the flail of wind and cold. He paused a moment, tugged once at the peak of his greasy cap and edged inside.

Four moth-eaten pool tables were picked out by the strong white light that tunneled down from low-swung lamps. Two tables were busy. A stout man in a brown sweater was leaning his elbows on a grimy glass tobacco-counter beside the door. He lifted his eyes and grunted:

"Hello, Baldy."

Wentworth sneezed, dragged a limp handkerchief from his pocket.

" 'Lo," he snuffled. He was counting on the faked cold to turn aside any suspicions of his voice. "Where's McSwag?"

The man's eyes showed the whites under the irises as he looked up again. "Back room," he said slowly.

Wentworth shuffled that way. The men at the tables had stopped playing and were watching him with unshifting eyes. The Spider knew their faces, killers all. His shoulders seemed to cringe even more. He snuffled and bobbed the big dome of his head.

"Hello," he said.

Not one of them spoke. Wentworth's mind was racing behind

the half-frightened mask of his disguise. Was it possible there had been some split between McSwag and the Master that he didn't know about? Was he betraying his masquerade by coming here? But that seemed unlikely. The man at the door had addressed him as Baldy, and that indicated his identity at least was accepted. Something was wrong, though. He knew that. The

The spidery span of Brooklyn Bridge was falling to the black water below!

place was too quiet and too noisy by turns. The rough laughter that burst out now and then from the restaurant seemed to have an edge.

Wentworth snuffled and eased into the back room. All his

movements had the frightened air that went with the character of Baldy. Ram Singh had noticed that the man was at once cringing and insolent in his dealings with Hackerson. As if he feared the man personally and yet knew that somehow he held a whip hand. Such was Wentworth's air tonight as he went into the back room and looked about for McSwag. He knew the Irishman by sight, a roundly solid mountain of strength, with a craggy head that might have set upon the shoulders of some ancient Iberian king. And McSwag was a king in his own territory. Politicians hastened to do him favors and police wore a worried look when something came up that involved his powerful mob.

McSwag was not visible in the back room and Wentworth slipped around a battered table where men played monosyllabic poker. The four looked up as the supposed Baldy went by and the dealer stopped flipping cards to lift his eyes beneath a green shade. A white cone of light burned down and left their faces mostly in shadow.

Wentworth sneezed twice violently. "Where's McSwag?" he asked.

The dealer said nastily, "What do you care?"

Wentworth seemed to shrink by inches, but his pinched mouth tightened a little. "I'll tell McSwag that," he whined. "And don't get ideas in your head, Hickey, that just because I'm not a hood...."

Hickey slammed his chair back and came around the table with long strides. Wentworth did not cringe any longer. He stood still and the tight mouth grinned slightly. Hickey stopped two feet short of him uncertainly and Wentworth sniggered.

"Go on, hit me," he said.

Hickey cursed and spun back to his chair. "I'll let McSwag tend to you," he growled. "Go on and see him."

"Where is he?" Wentworth insisted.

"Up on Brooklyn Bridge, waiting for it to fall," Hickey flung at him. He picked up the cards and started to deal again.

The other men were grinning.

WENTWORTH TURNED toward the door he had entered. "It's okay by me," he said. "You can tell McSwag I was here with a message and you ran me away."

"Aw, for the love of Pete, Baldy," Hickey growled. "You know damned well McSwag is upstairs in his office. What's the idea of the gag?" The statement was accompanied by a sideways jerk of the head and Wentworth saw a black doorway in the dark shadows of a corner.

Wentworth sneezed, cursed and shuffled toward the stairs. His confidence was mounting. All these men held Baldy in contempt, but they were a little afraid of him, a little uncertain just what he could command in the way of protection. He stumbled up the dark stairs found a door under which a thread of light glowed. Voices were mumbled inside. He knocked and pushed in.

A skinny man jumped up from a chair against the wall, a gun flashed in his hand.

"Why in hell don't you wait till you're asked in?" he snarled.

"Go count bugs!" Wentworth cursed at him, even while his shoulders cringed.

He flashed a glance over the room and barely caught the start that jerked at his muscles. Jackson and a man who looked like a detective were seated, bound hand and foot, against the wall. The detective's face was bloody, and the muscles sat out in knots along Jackson's wide Gascon jaws. Wentworth turned his surprise into a sneer and turned confidentially toward the man who sat unmoved across the room, ensconced in a big easy chair before a gas log that filled the room with a sweetly-sickening heat. The man was McSwag and his little blue eyes, like small hard marbles under the low bushing of his brows, were on Wentworth. Seated beside him, twisted toward him with her hand arrested, apparently in the middle of an emphatic gesture, was Beatrice Ross, the girl friend of the man Wentworth had killed, Devil Hackerson.

Her face was dead white except for the vivid gash of her mouth. A mink coat was tossed across the back of her chair and her crossed legs caught the fire gleam on their silk. Two empty whiskey glasses and a bottle sat on a taborette between the man and woman.

Gang etiquette demanded that Wentworth ask no questions about the prisoners and he ignored them. It was clear enough that they had been caught trailing the Ross woman. The detective doubtless was Kirkpatrick's man.

"Where's the dough?" McSwag demanded coldly. He looked as solid as Gibraltar in the chair and there was an impression of leashed ferocity about the man. He didn't move, just sat there staring at Wentworth.

"The Master says…" Wentworth began with a whine.

"He ain't got no dough," the man by the door said shrilly.

McSwag's eyes swung toward him a moment and the voice died. He looked back to Wentworth.

"It'll be ready tomorrow," Wentworth went on, stopped to sneeze. "The Master says to turn the girl loose."

"You may tell this bozo you call the Master," said McSwag, "to go to hell!"

The slouched shoulders of the false Baldy jerked in a little shrug. "I'll tell him if you says so." He cringed. "But if I do there ain't going to be no more of the 'stuff' for youse."

McSwag was abruptly on his feet. There was no preliminary tightening of muscles that Wentworth could perceive—no hands thrusting against the chair arms. He simply straightened his legs and was on his feet. It was proof of the heavy strength of his mountainous body. He reached Wentworth in a stride and seized his shoulder.

"You little rat," he snarled.

Beatrice Ross got slowly to her feet. Her pink tongue touched the burning red of her lips. "Hit him, Mickey," she urged eagerly. FOR A moment, McSwag seemed about to obey, his eyes glaring down at Wentworth. But though the Spider's body seemed to shrivel in fear, his eyes met those of the gangster chieftain directly. McSwag thrust him abruptly back, strode to his chair. He did not seat himself again, however.

"I ain't got nothing to do with it, McSwag," Wentworth

131

protested. "I'm just a lobbygow, a windbag for the guy what calls himself the Master. I ain't even seen him and I'm just telling you what he says. He says turn the girl loose or you don't get any more of the 'stuff.'"

McSwag swore violently. "So he's going to get hard, is he? Okay, that's a game I can deal cards in, too. You tell him."

Beatrice Ross sidled forward and plucked at his sleeve. McSwag moved his arm impatiently, but she persisted.

"Listen, Mickey," she said tightly. "This guy ain't Baldy."

Wentworth put a puzzled look on his face, sneezed in the middle of it McSwag said, "What the hell?"

"I'm telling you," said the woman vehemently. "Baldy is short'n this guy, and Baldy ain't had a cold all winter. I think this guy is faking that cold to hide his voice."

McSwag said, "So!" His voice was soft and his eyes became round. He came forward on the balls of his feet and Wentworth felt a gun gouge suddenly into his back.

"You're nuts," he protested shrilly. "I say you're nuts!"

The door banged open suddenly and McSwag jerked up his head and stared past Wentworth. He tried to twist around also, but the man jabbed harder with the gun muzzle and he stopped trying. He heard startled exclamations behind him, then a squeaky voice a whole lot like the one he had assumed.

"So you got him already, have you, McSwag?" the voice said.

Shuffling footsteps approached and a face peered into his own, a face with a cast in one eye, a face smoking a cigarette and shadowed by the peak of a greasy cap. Beneath that cap-edge no hair showed. It was Baldy.

Wentworth still look puzzled. "Who the hell are you?" he growled. "Watcha doing made up to look like me?"

Baldy dragged off his cap.

"Okay, Hickey," he sniggered. "You tell which is the real Baldy."

Wentworth's cap was dragged off and a rough hand ran over his head. The poker player of the green eye-shade stepped to his side and put the other hand on Baldy's head, gripped with his fingers. Wentworth felt the man's fingers denting the false scalp on his head, knew that it was only a matter of seconds before it was ripped from his head and his real identity was revealed. The gun gouged harder into his back, McSwag's marble eyes were fixed on him with flat, cold menace and behind him there were at least three other men. Beatrice Ross stared at him and slowly her eyes widened.

"I know who this guy is," she gasped. "It's… My God! *It's the Spider!*"

CHAPTER 13
"LET ME KILL HIM!"

HICKEY SHOVED and tugged at the false bald head that Ram Singh had fastened on Wentworth's scalp. It hurt, but it held. Ram Singh had done his work well. Hickey cursed and quit

"I can't get it off," he said, "but this guy isn't Baldy. That's a fake head on there, and…."

McSwag stepped in close and his right fist swept up. It was

133

aimed at the jaw, but Wentworth jerked his head, took the blow high up on his cheek. Nevertheless he went down hard and a great white burst of light smashed through his brain. Dully he felt shoes thud against his sides, felt the sharp heel of Beatrice Ross rake the side of his face.

Fumbling, he reached for his guns. There wasn't much feeling in his hands. Before they had moved six inches, fists pinioned his wrists to the floor. His guns were ripped from their holsters. More heels hit his sides. His stomach seemed caved in. Then he was aware of a big figure over him and fists flailing.

"Lay off!" McSwag bellowed, "You can have him in a minute. First I want to ask some questions. Lay off, I say!"

Wentworth felt himself dragged up and slammed into a chair. Whiskey burned down his throat. Water drenched him. He gasped, rolled his head and came foggily back to his senses. McSwag was holding Beatrice Ross away from him with an arm like a limb of oak. Behind him were four men and insane hatred glared from their eyes. Baldy hovered to one side, a smirking grin on his face. And Wentworth saw death in all those faces, even in the grim, hard face of McSwag who, he realized dimly, had saved him from being beaten to death a few moments before.

The Spider could expect no mercy here. Not a criminal in the entire country but had come to dread and hate his name as that of the one man who could strike terror into their hearts. Not a man in this group but who, some time, had been blocked and defeated in criminal endeavor by some crusade of the Spider. His lethal guns had burned down their companions. Now they had him a helpless prisoner! Jackson and the detective were equally useless.

"I just want to know who this Spider guy is," McSwag said, "then you can have him. Now lay off a minute, will you?"

"He killed Devil Hackerson," Beatrice Ross screeched, "and I'm going to kill him!"

"Sure, sure," McSwag soothed. "Now wait!"

The woman kept struggling to get past his arm and he drew back his hand and hit her hard with the heel. She spun up against the wall and struck it with her shoulders. Her head snapped back and she slid down slowly, a dazed look in her eyes.

"Let me kill him!" she moaned.

McSwag ignored her, turned back to Wentworth. The other men waited, tensely, leashed hounds at the kill, dogs beaten back after tasting blood. They licked their lips and fingered their weapons.

"Your number's up, Spider," McSwag said slowly. "You were a damn' fool to come here like this. And this is once you ain't going to wiggle out of it Come on, who are you?"

WENTWORTH LIFTED his head from the back of the chair. He realized he was in the big arm seat that McSwag had occupied. It was an effective prison, for he was bedded so deeply in it that there was no chance for him to move any way but forward. McSwag and his four men hedged him in there. There was no chance to tip the chair over backward either. It was too heavy for that. Besides, that beating had done him up.

He dipped his hands into his vest pocket for his cigarette-case

135

and McSwag knocked it from his hand. It snapped against the gas log with a silvery note.

"I just wanted a smoke," Wentworth explained mildly.

"Okay," McSwag grunted, "but you'll smoke *my* cigarettes. Get the point?"

"Oh, quite," said Wentworth. He accepted one of McSwag's cigarettes and lighted it. "Quite," he said, "You seem to have me at a temporary disadvantage."

"Temporary is right," McSwag growled and a grudging admiration lighted his eyes. "It's going to last about two minutes and then the disadvantage is going to become permanent. Come on, now, who are you?"

"The Master knows," Beatrice Ross said suddenly. "He had him followed, and ordered a train wrecked to get him."

McSwag said, "That ain't helping. I wrecked the train and I don't know who he is. You know, Baldy?"

Baldy licked his lips. "I'll tell you," he said hoarsely, "if you'll let me kill him."

McSwag looked at him in surprise.

"You?" he demanded.

There was a crazy gleam in Baldy's one good eye. He nodded his head. "Yeah, I want to blow off that funny-looking head."

Wentworth laughed. "Really, Baldy," he said, "it wasn't such a bad head until Hickey started mussing it up."

For the first time he saw a gleam of hope. Baldy was no hood, didn't know how to handle a gun. If he could goad the man into making an attempt, he might stand a chance of snatching the weapon. It was certain Baldy would come dose to use it. He glanced out of the corner of his masked eyes toward the cigarette case. It was beginning to melt a little with the gas-log's heat.

"Let me!" Baldy pleaded.

"No!" Beatrice Ross said violently. "I'm going to." She stopped suddenly, snatched up her skirt and yanked a small gun from a thigh holster. Before she could use it McSwag had wrenched it from her hand.

McSwag weighed Beatrice's gun on his hand and eyed Baldy. "I think that might be a good idea," he said softly. There was a gleam in his eyes. Wentworth could read his thoughts. If he had a murder he could hold over Baldy's head, he might twist him to his own ends, use him against the Master. The Spider blew another smoke ring and was thankful that the Zeiss lenses hid the mounting hope in his eyes.

"Shoot him in the belly, Baldy," Hickey urged hoarsely. "I want to put lead in him, too. He smashed out Trigger Skinner, and…."

"Now, boys, boys," McSwag urged jovially. "I see no reason why all of you shouldn't have a shot. The Spider isn't going to run away, are you, Spider?"

Wentworth smiled and carefully blew another ring. "Oh, no!" he said calmly. "I wouldn't cheat you out of your fun."

It was an effort to keep his face twisted into that mocking smile. His heart was a hard thing beating against the wall of his ribs, trying to knock its way out. In his right temple, the thin scar was throbbing. He knew that never before had he been so near death as now. He knew that never had he needed more to live, not only for his own sake, but for the sake of the thousands these men would kill if he died.

DESPITE ALL his battling, he still did not know the Master. And ten thousand lives might well hinge on his escape....

"I think Baldy ought to have first shot," McSwag said, "because the Spider came here disguised as him."

He held the gun out to Baldy butt first. Baldy snatched for it and at the same instant, Beatrice Ross catapulted upward from the floor, hands clawing for the weapon. McSwag roared out with anger, stepped forward to interfere, and his bulk spun Baldy aside. The little windbag had the gun and he clutched it in both hands reeling back. Wentworth dived out of the chair and his shoulder caught him in the side.

Baldy spun, felt the heat of the gas log and screamed. Wentworth snatched the gun away from him, blasted one slug from it at Hickey, who alone was in the clear, and a second later made the protection of the heavy chair. Hickey took the bullet between the eyes and slammed down onto the floor, clawing the rug. His gun skated along and Wentworth snatched it from behind the chair. Deliberately he shot down another hood, then smacked out the light with two more bullets.

McSwag had dropped to the floor with the first shot and the big chair was between him and Wentworth. His heavy gun roared and lead plunked through the back of the chair—within an inch of the Spider's head! Wentworth lay flat on the floor and burned lead along the level of the boards. McSwag swore painfully and more bullets smacked into the chair. Two came through.

A small, muffled blast *whooshed* near the gas log as his ciga-rette case exploded and Wentworth laughed. It was the mocking monotone of the Spider's mirth. "Death!" he cackled. "Death! The Spider brings you death!"

Beatrice Ross was screaming with pain now. "Tear gas!" she shrieked. "Tear gas!"

Wentworth caught a movement in the flickering light of the gas log and fired into it twice. A man groaned and thudded to the floor. Wentworth was edging along the wall toward the door. Somewhere in this room, Baldy still crouched. There was still another gunman, Beatrice Ross and McSwag. McSwag was wounded, but Wentworth doubted that he was dead. Also, there was a pounding of feet on the stairway as the men down-stairs rushed upward to the rescue. Wentworth reached the door, yanked it open. From the darkness of the room, a gun blazed wildly, and the Spider's own eyes, even protected as they were by the Zeiss lenses, were smarting with the tear gas his ciga-rette case had released, but the bullet did not come anywhere near him. He must free Jackson, but to do that he must empty the room.

He plunged out into the hall, squealing wildly as he ran toward the stairs. "The Spider! The Spider!" he squeaked. And once more it was Baldy's voice.

A rush of men whirled him sidewise against the wall. The man who had stood behind the counter pinned him there by his coat collar, peering at him in the dim light from the hall's single bulb. Other men dashed by. The man cursed.

"You ain't the real Baldy," he growled and his gun jerked

139

upward at his side. Wentworth fired upward and the bullet smashed under the man's chin, thrust his head back between his shoulder blades. He went back two heavy steps on his heels, already dead, then fell limply. Wentworth crouched low, leaped the entire flight of steps, landed sprawling and rolled as a hurricane of flying lead ploughed the floor where he had landed.

WENTWORTH EMPTIED the light gun up the stairs, then darted out of the store. He reached his car in a bound, flung into it and kicked the starter. A mighty creaking sound, a Titan in agony, suddenly filled all the world. There was a whang of steel as if a great wire cable had been cut by a bullet. With an abrupt stab of dread, Wentworth ducked forward over the wheel, stared upward.

The spidery span of Brooklyn Bridge, with its myriad tiny lights, was sagging. A splotch of glaring white headlights stabbed wildly downward, then spun dizzily, whirling through space toward the black waters. An automobile was plunging from the bridge. But it was not alone. An entire string of elevated cars tumbled like a child's toy train down after it.

Brooklyn Bridge was falling…!

Good God! The Master and his steel-eater had destroyed the Brooklyn Bridge!

Even as the thought materialized into words, a bunch of men hurdled out the front door of the restaurant, guns in hands. They froze there. Their heads twisted, too, toward that catastrophe of the bridge.

His lips grinning back from his teeth, Wentworth realized that the engine of his coupé was racing. With a snarl of fury, he yanked the car into gear, deliberately charged the six men on the walk.

He was within feet of them before they tore their eyes away from the death they had wrought. Their wild screams and upflung guns, attempted to stem the rush of the steel monster whose driver had become an avenging demon. Their bullets were as futile as their screams. The car struck two of them down, slammed them savagely to the concrete, ground another against the wall, charged on to carry two more through the plate glass window of the restaurant.

One of them tore loose. He clapped his hands to his back and ran screaming down the street. Blood flowed from his back in a torrent. He did not run far. Wentworth threw back his head and laughed—a sound of blood-curdling merriment....

CHAPTER 14
McSWAG PAYS

WENTWORTH WAS numb with horror at the slaughter these men had wrought; he was choked with rage that his swift retribution had not calmed. He smothered his wild laughter, flung from the coupé and swiftly snatched two guns from among the crushed corpses on the pavement. One still-moaning victim spotted Wentworth and lifted a heavy gun. Without compunction, the Spider smashed a bullet through his head. He busied himself a moment, pressing his crimson seals upon the foreheads of his prey, then, automatic in either fist, he slipped back into the pool-room. Once more his lips were snarling his bitter hatred.

From the adjoining restaurant, people had poured in a noisy, frightened flood. The gangsters from the poolroom were either dead in the street or smashed down by Wentworth's bullets upstairs. But McSwag and Baldy were still in the battle and Jackson remained to be rescued. The Spider was a silent shadow flitting through the pool-room, up those dark back stairs. Excited voices and McSwag's coldly venomous tones floated down to him. He went past the sweatered man he had slain and upon him, too, he left his seal.

"Damn it," McSwag's raging voice came to him as he stooped beside the corpse. "Get me out of here and get the girl out, too. Police can't hold off on this. There's been too much shooting. We'll gain some time because that Brooklyn Bridge smash will pull most of the cops away...."

Wentworth drifted to a spot where he could peer into the room, saw Beatrice Ross and a gangster supporting McSwag. Baldy had vanished. The Spider's eyes tightened. His lips were stiff with rage. This was the man who had wrecked the train, who had wrecked the bridge, plunging a thousand innocents to death, maiming thousands more. The Spider went in behind his guns. Beatrice Ross screamed—a long shrill cry—and sprang back. The gangster reeled away from McSwag's side, hand darting for his gun. With his eyes still on McSwag, the Spider sped a single bullet that smashed the hood to the floor. He did it as a man might swat an annoying fly.

McSwag staggered when the two sprang from his side, but

he braced himself on his wounded leg. "I haven't any gun," he stammered.

"I know it," said Wentworth. He shot McSwag's other leg out from under him, dropped the man cursing to the floor.

Beatrice Ross was spread-eagled against the wall, her palms beating in frenzy. She was too terrified to make a sound. The Spider's face was a mask of avenging fury. His automatic's muzzle was centered now on McSwag's stomach.

"Don't, for God's sake!" McSwag screamed. "You wouldn't kill a helpless man!"

The Spider laughed again and McSwag stammered into blood-chilled silence. McSwag knew that he had given those men and women on the train and bridge no chance. They had been struck down in helpless impotence. Why should he…? Wentworth's finger tightened slowly on the trigger. A thought stopped him. This man alone among the living knew where Betty Briggs was held prisoner.

"Lift your hands above your head, Jackson," Wentworth said, forcing words between his tight lips.

Jackson stretched out his bound hands, the wrists straining apart and the Spider fired twice carefully. Jackson strained and his bullet-burned bonds parted. He went to work on his feet, then began to untie the detective.

"McSwag," Wentworth's voice sounded rusty. "I'll give you one chance. Tell me where Betty Briggs is and instead of killing you, I'll turn you over to the police."

Hope flared in McSwag's eyes. "She's upstairs," he said swiftly, "in the room at the end of the hall."

AT A nod from Wentworth, Jackson stumbled, feet numb from the bonds, out into the hall. The others waited. Beatrice Ross had ceased to beat the wall. She was crouched, her hennaed hair a-sprawl on her shoulders. Her too-full lips looked bloody with their carmine. McSwag breathed heavily through his mouth, his eyes fixed with fearful fascination on the hard, unyielding face of the Spider. The detective was untying his feet with numb fingers and he, too, watched Wentworth warily. He was not quite sure what to expect from this killer who single-handed had smashed the most dangerous mob of the city, but at least his intentions seemed friendly. His fellow prisoner had been released and had immediately unbound his hands for him. He stopped to flex his fingers, began to work again on the ropes and Jackson came back to the doorway, a girl's quick-heeled patter beside him.

He did not look toward her. "Jackson, take Miss Briggs to the street. I'll join you in a moment."

McSwag's face was gray. "You promised! You promised!" he stammered.

Wentworth took two long strides toward him and the gang leader flung his arms over his face protectingly. The Spider's gun lashed down and McSwag's arms dropped. The sounds that came from his throat no longer formed words. They were scarcely human. There was a swift gleam of metal and Wentworth retreated quick steps, a mocking smile twisted his lips. McSwag's trembling hands lifted to his forehead in bewilderment.

"He's branded you, Mickey!" Beatrice Ross gasped hoarsely. "Branded you with his seal!" McSwag's hands whipped away from his forehead. The seal was a bloody smear on his pallid face. "The next time I see you," the Spider said softly. "I'm going to put a bullet right through the center of my seal."

He backed toward the door, flicked a glance toward the detective and saw the man lurch to his feet.

"Okay, officer?" he asked him.

"Okay," the man nodded.

"Catch!" Wentworth tossed him an automatic. The detective's hands and eyes flew toward it. When he looked up, the gun tight in his fist, the doorway was empty. Mocking flat laughter drifted back through the darkness. Seated on the floor, his two legs in a widening pool of blood, McSwag began to curse with a terrible, rasp-throated vehemence. His mob was killed off. He was wounded and in the hands of police, and that brand on his forehead would make him forever a mockery and a butt of gangster laughter.

IN THE street outside, Jackson had backed the coupé clear of the bodies on the walk and had the motor running. Wentworth crowded in beside the girl without a word and the car swung in a U-curve and buffeted the wind at an inconspicuous speed. Wentworth was feeling the reaction of his burning anger now. He was limp, empty inside. He turned his head heavily toward Betty Briggs and found her curious eyes on his face. The eyes were green and wanted to be merry; her bare head was a tangle of dark red curls.

"I'd like to call Daddums," she said, "as soon as you can let me, Spider."

"He knows already that you're safe," he assured her. "It will be tomorrow before you can call him. Jackson, take Miss Briggs to the hideout you know of. Don't let anyone see you go in. Stay there and wait for word from me. Drop me at the next subway station."

He descended and caught a loafing local train, sank back in a corner with his eyes closed. Kirkpatrick would be at the scene of the bridge wreck, of course. He glanced at his watch and saw that the *Berengaria* had sailed an hour before. Nita, at least, was out of harm's way. Within a few days there should be some word of this mysterious Butterworth. He wondered if Alrecht had been captured, and his mind switched to McSwag. Twice now, he had shattered the gangs that obeyed the Master's orders. Would he organize again? Or would he deem the work of popularizing Bessmo steel complete, and rest content on his achievements?

A hard smile twisted Wentworth's mouth. The answer to that lay in the destruction of Brooklyn Bridge. The Master was not yet through! More thousands were to die and other thousands go through life as cripples to fill his pockets.

Wentworth discarded his disguise in a washroom, went to his apartment for clothing, gave some instructions, then hurried to police headquarters. Kirkpatrick had just returned wearily from the wreckage of Brooklyn Bridge. Pounds seemed to have been stripped from his lean body, years added to his shoulders. He dropped behind his desk without waiting to remove coat or derby. He looked beaten.

"Briggs got off all right," he said heavily. "Didn't want to go, but I think it was wise to get him out of the country before we make the announcement about Bessmo steel. The president of Bessmo convinced me it would do what it's supposed to."

Wentworth reached for a phone and put in a call to Professor Brownlee.

"Where'd you send Briggs?" he asked Kirkpatrick.

"Put him on the *Berengaria.*" The Commissioner was fingering through some reports distractedly and frowned at Wentworth's laughter. "What's the matter?" he demanded.

"Nothing at all," Wentworth said. "I sent Nita abroad on the same boat."

Kirkpatrick smiled wanly. "There were a number of last minute passengers. Briggs wouldn't go unless Nancy Collins went along as his secretary. Nancy wouldn't go unless her brother-in-law, Anse, was with her. Luckily, Anse called us here to report he hadn't been able to find Alrecht and we got hold of him. He tried to dissuade Nancy, but finally went."

Wentworth frowned. He had counted on Anse Collins' help in his activities of the next few days, but it couldn't be helped now.

"Damn it," he swore. "Everything is going haywire. Still no trace of Baldy, I suppose?"

THE PHONE rang. Professor Brownlee agreed to call the newspapers and give them the information on Bessmo steel. "I haven't been able to find a way to make steel impervious to crystallizing," he said, "but gold-plating might prevent any external attack."

Wentworth had scarcely hung up when the phone buzzed again. He frowned, picking up the receiver, then handed the instrument to Kirkpatrick with a quizzical grimace. "For you," he said and watched Kirkpatrick's face grow in turns angry and puzzled as he listened.

"You turn that girl loose," Kirkpatrick barked. "Do you hear…?" He jiggled the hook up and down in vain, roared out an order to trace the call. He hung up, turned baffled eyes to Wentworth.

"That was the Spider," he said slowly. "I'll swear it was. He had the same mocking laugh, the same flat expressionless voice and the slightly pedantic manner of speech. Damn it, Dick, quit playing tricks on me. I'm in no gay mood."

Wentworth raised questioning eyebrows. "Aside from the matter of tricks, which I'm not playing," he said, "what in the hell are you talking about?"

"The Spider…." said Kirkpatrick, then hesitated, "the Spider informs me that he has freed Betty Briggs, that when I need her to testify against McSwag he'll produce her, but in the meantime he's keeping her safe himself. "I didn't know McSwag had been arrested," he said slowly. "I see the Spider has stolen the march on me once more. He killed nine gangsters. He desired me to know, over the phone, that the reason we hadn't been able to trace Betty's phone call was that it had come over a tapped-in phone."

He stared at Wentworth, but his friend's face gave no hint of the amusement he felt. He had instructed Jackson to make the call and imitate the Spider's voice, no difficult trick since the voice was a false tone to begin with, a deliberately disguised chest voice whose chief characteristic was its mockery and its monotone. Although Kirkpatrick believed that he was the Spider, it was just as well to shake that belief on occasion—to give him reason to deny to his superiors and his men that Wentworth and the Spider were one and be able to cite proof of it.

"It's fantastic, Dick," Kirkpatrick said. He shrugged. "I think I'll resign in favor of... the Spider!" He grinned.

Suddenly the teletype machine in the corner of the office which brought in reports from other boroughs and states began to clatter. There was excitement in its swift, rattling clicks, so much so that Kirkpatrick's eyes jerked to the instrument and Wentworth twisted about to stare. Both men sprang to their feet and raced to the instrument. It ticked out:

U.S.S. CRUISER PENNSYNAPOLIS SUNK... ALL ABOARD BELIEVED LOST... STEEL SIDES BROKE IN WHEN CURRENT SLAMMED SHIP AGAINST PIER.

Wentworth went rigid, his hands clenched. Kirkpatrick's hoarse voice rasped out oaths in an unrecognizable tone. "By God!" he swore, and his voice became solemn. "If I catch the Master, I shall torture him to death!"

Wentworth stared at his friend's pale, drawn face and knew that Kirkpatrick had pronounced a solemn pledge he would never fulfill—not if the Spider could fulfill it first!

CHAPTER 15
A STRONG MAN FAKERS

I N THE days that followed, Wentworth fought a battle that was strange for the Spider. Instead of fighting in the night against the Master's men, he devoted himself to devising safety measures that would cut down the fearful toll of lives, directing the efforts of a hundred detectives whom Kirkpatrick placed under his personal direction. This was no time for smashing through lines of gangsters. Twice now, the Spider had wiped out mobs, and still the slaughter of the innocents went on. He must, in this case, run down the leader and eliminate him. When that was done, the gangs could be wiped out to some purpose.

The slaughter went on relentlessly. Bridges were smashed. Buildings tumbled into the streets. Ships shook their plates to pieces in the battering of the Atlantic gales. Trains found rails dissolving under their swift wheels and spilled pitiful dead across the countryside, but gradually the number of deaths diminished, though the wreckage continued. The rigid regulations set up in New York under Wentworth's administration and copied throughout the East began to take effect.

Still buildings continued to crash to the streets and bridges collapsed beneath puny loads. Cities were deserted by every man and woman who could possibly escape, fleeing to the rural areas where steel was not used for building. Men who had to remain sent their wives and children away. Going to work, they walked in the middle of the street with fearful eyes continually alert for the first hint of a building's collapse. On windy days, all shops and offices closed.

Such was the city that New York had become—in which the Spider fought to save human lives. When he had done all that he possibly could to check the mounting toll of the steel-eater, Wentworth pushed on with his investigations. He heard from Nita that though Butterworth had been traced to England through his passport, his family had seen nothing of him. Alrecht had not been found. Briggs was clamoring for permission to come home and petition the Spider for the return of his daughter. Finally, he declared he would defy Kirkpatrick's advice and start on the *Britannia*, England's newest and swiftest ship.

The police had checked the list of Bessmo stock holders without finding anyone suspicious save Alrecht, but Wentworth was not satisfied. He went over the list himself and looked up the private history of each man. Then he paid each a personal visit and in that way finally came to O'Leary Simpson. That man, newspaper clippings had told him, had built a school building ten years before that had collapsed and killed half a hundred children. He had been cleared of blame by an inquiry. Furthermore, Wentworth's interview with him had yielded nothing. He went from the man's office to a newspaper and went to the clipping files, the Morgue as it is called.

Wentworth frowned over the clipping about O'Leary Simpson. It was foolish to suppose there was any connection between that happening so long ago and these modern tragedies. Yet the man was in a position to profit largely by the mounting sale of Bessmo steel, which was being turned out by carloads in a triple-shift factory. Hundreds of other steel factories all over the country were paying for the privilege of installing the Bessmo process in their mills. And O'Leary Simpson was next to the largest holder of stock in the Bessmo corporation, which, Wentworth was sure was the key to this whole tragic enigma. He got up slowly from the table where he had been reading the clippings and his jaw tensed in resolve.

Wentworth would pay O'Leary Simpson another visit, but this time it would be the Spider who called.

THE HEAVY twilight was thick as Wentworth pushed his way out into a windy, rain-swept street. Men walked behind wind-buffeted umbrellas in the middle of the street. Asphalt glistened with the watery trail of the few moving headlights. A bit early for the Spider's call… He turned up his coat collar, thrust his head into the whipping drops. He could not recall a single war with the underworld's master minds that had defied him so many weeks. There had been some in which, on the verge of conquering, he had been laid low by wounds. There had been times when a prison cell had kept him from the battle. But it was none of these in the present case. He simply had been unable to run the Master to earth.

Alrecht, upon whom his suspicions centered, had disappeared as utterly as if his body had been pulped in the crash of one of the skyscrapers, ground into a bloody unrecognizable slime as had been so many thousands of the population of the East. Baldy had not been sighted again, but the evidences of his work were everywhere.

Wentworth turned his heavy footsteps toward home, let

Jenkyns take his soggy coat and hat. With an effort he braced his shoulders, lifted his head. The Spider was not beaten, could not be beaten, he told himself. For the sake of suffering humanity to which he long ago had dedicated his life and service, he must succeed.

The phone rang and Wentworth was electrified at Nita's first words. She said breathlessly: "We have found Butterworth, but he refuses to return with us."

Wentworth threw back his head and laughed, feeling new life within him. "Then kidnap him!" he said. "Bring him back on the *Britannia*, sailing tomorrow noon. Here's how you can do it." He swiftly outlined a simple plan in which Ram Singh's make-up ability would figure. Butterworth would seem a helpless invalid, in care of the Hindu and Nita.

"I have evidence," said Nita, "that Butterworth has been in constant communication with America. He has made some heavy deposits in banks, all in the name of Alrecht."

Wentworth laughed again, and jubilance crept into his voice, "It looks, my beloved, as if you have gone the Spider one better this time," he told her, "and are solving this mystery all by yourself. By the way, Briggs is coming back on the *Britannia*, and that means Nancy Collins and Anse. You won't lack company."

Hanging up the phone, Wentworth strode across the music room to the organ, stepped up until he could reach the vents of two treble pipes. He tapped their edges with a rhythmic, alternate cadence and they made dim echoes of notes. He paused, went through the cadence again, then stepped down. A tapestry-covered panel in the side wall pivoted soundlessly outward, a yellow glow sprang up within.

HE STRODE into the yellow glow and with a dim click the panel revolved again and closed behind him. Within the narrow room beyond, Wentworth swiftly assumed the disguise of the Spider, lank hair and beak nose, cape and black hat and hunched back. This room was a recent installation, necessitated by the increasing frequency with which public suspicion centered upon himself as the Spider—by the occasional forays of police. He had bought the entire apartment building, had the suite below his vacated and Professor Brownlee and himself had made the necessary changes in the walls.

When they finished their work, his apartment would become an impregnable fortress, but so far there was only this dressing room and a hidden exit into the service-stairs by way of a porter's closet in the hall. Within ten minutes, Wentworth was stealing down the stairs, letting himself out into the dark street where the rain still bounced shattered drops from glistening pavements. It was turning colder. Wentworth drew the cape tightly about him and entered a battered old coupé whose disreputable hood masked a powerful engine. This, too, was a camouflage that had been forced upon him.

He fought the cold engine to life and sped northward, swinging presently into Central Park, crossing the 155th Street Bridge over the Harlem ship canal and taking the Grand Concourse with its row on row of white-faced apartment houses. O'Leary Simpson lived in Bronxville, a small, exclusive suburb within ten miles of the city limits. As Wentworth had planned it, he would arrive there shortly after midnight. Unless the Simpsons had guests, they should be in bed then, which suited the Spider's plans excellently.

The house was a sprawling Spanish style dwelling, smooth white walls and roof of tile. Wentworth coasted past it and saw no lights, whirled, a corner and parked. His approach was as silent as his shadow. He searched for and found the burglar alarm on a window and attached to its two plates a length of wire. The alarm was of the type that sounded a gong when a plate on the window and another on the frame were separated, thus breaking a circuit. By means of the wire, he prevented that happening. He shut the window soundlessly behind him, unlocked a side door with the same caution, then crept up broad marble stairs to the second floor. Silently, he visited every door along the hall, located persons sleeping behind three of them: one, the daughter; another, the wife; the third, O'Leary Simpson.

At that door, he listened longest, and satisfied that the man slept, he entered. The connecting door between the rooms of the man and his wife was open and this the Spider shut; then he crossed to Simpson's side. He weighed a black-jack upon his palm and then struck lightly just behind the sleeping man's ear. The rhythm of Simpson's breathing broke for a moment, his muscles jerked, then relaxed. His breathing continued, a little more shallow and roughened, that was all.

Wentworth whipped back the covers, rolled a blanket about the unconscious man and heaved him up to his shoulder with a smooth ease that spoke volumes for the strength of those broad, athletic shoulders. As silently as he had entered, he descended, slid out the door he had prepared below and went rapidly to his car. He handcuffed Simpson to a nickeled ring beside the seat, installed for just that purpose, and drove quietly away.

He opened the window a little on Simpson's side and after ten minutes of cold wind, the man began to squirm in his seat, moaned jerkily. Suddenly he sat bolt upright. The abrupt motion made him moan again and attempt to raise his hands to his head. The handcuffs grated on the nickeled ring and he stared at them dazedly, then whipped his head around toward the driver. The Spider did not look at him. His hunched back beneath the black cape, his sallow face glowing in the dim—light, made a sinister picture. O'Leary Simpson's breath came swiftly.

THE SPIDER said nothing. He knew that uncertainty would work more damage on Simpson's morale than any threats he could make. And he must break Simpson's courage to make him talk. If he was involved, it should not be difficult. This man had gone to bed in the security of his home, an expensive home which his wealth had built. He awoke, apparently from that sleep, to find himself riding through a wild night, handcuffed, and seated beside a sinister, black-draped figure. He would think at first that it was a nightmare....

"Who are you?" Simpson demanded in a voice that vainly strove to be angry. His voice gained strength. "Who are you and what the hell do you mean by this?" His handcuffs rattled.

The Spider turned his head slowly, looked with cold implacable hatred into Simpson's eyes, so that the man winced back into his corner. Then the Spider looked back to the road. He didn't

156

say anything, and neither did Simpson for a long while. The car rattled its way to the end of the Bronx River Parkway, took the sharp grade to the right of Kensico dam at forty-five. The engine made only a slight hissing. The rain drummed.

"In God's name," Simpson asked hoarsely. "Who are you? Why are you doing this to me?"

This time the Spider did not even turn his head. Simpson began to stammer out more questions, to threaten and curse, and finally to plead, but Wentworth ignored him. Finally the man fell silent, made little low moaning sounds that went on and on while the car reeled off ten miles, left the broad winding concrete highway that bordered the Kensico reservoir for a lonelier strip of macadam where the coupé jarred and rattled. The dash-light was improperly shielded and it turned the inside of the windshield into a dim mirror. In it Wentworth studied Simpson's face.

It was a fat, flaccid face, but beneath the blubber were the outlines of a hard and ruthless jaw. Simpson's mouth was lipless. It would be a straight gash in anger, but now it was trembling with weakness. A nervous *tic* quivered in the right corner. Simpson had an egg-shaped, partly bald head, colorless eyebrows, and there was a dewlap beneath his double chin. The dewlap quivered also.

The Spider's earlier elation of the evening was growing. Simpson's behavior had not been that of a guiltless man. Wentworth braked to a halt, leaned forward, cut the switch. Windshield-wiper and engine died together. The windshield clouded instantly with lashing drops that drummed like bony fingers along the roof and hammered on the tiny hood. Simpson was shaking all over. He watched Wentworth with furtive eyes. Suddenly he squealed. "Good God!" he cried. "I know you!… You… you're the…" his voice trailed off and the word Spider quaked from him in a quivering breath.

WENTWORTH TURNED his head slowly, his face expressionless. He slid a hand beneath his cape, a gesture of dread menace.

"Have you anything to say before…" Wentworth drew his hand slowly into view, showing the dull gleaming muzzle of an automatic.

"In God's name, Spider, I swear to you…" Simpson broke off, choking, as the muzzle of the gun swung slowly, centered on his body and lifted until he was staring with widening gaze down into the little black hole that was the eye of death. "I swear," he whimpered. "I'm getting nothing out of it at all."

The Spider's face did not change, but he knew now that he had guessed right, that O'Leary Simpson held a clue. He appeared to hesitate. His bitter blue-gray eyes stared along the barrel of his gun.

"My time is short," he said flatly. "You will have to talk fast, for if you fail to convince me by two o'clock…" A jerk of his head indicated the clock set into the rear vision mirror. It stood at three minutes of two. Simpson's eyes jumped to it, flew back to the face of the Spider. He licked his lips, sucked in a deep breath and began talking.

"I swear to you I didn't know what was behind it," he said rapidly. "Two months ago, a man called me over the telephone and reminded me that there existed written proof of a crime that would send me to prison for years...."

"You were responsible for the collapse of that school," Wentworth said softly. "They couldn't find your private set of specifications which told your foreman to shave the cement mixture, to use wood instead of steel, but this man could. He had the specifications. Who was this man?"

"I don't know," Simpson said. He whimpered suddenly and shrank back in his corner, tried to pull his manacled hands around in front of him as in prayer. "I don't know, Spider! As God is my witness!"

Wentworth had made no movement unless there was a slightly increased hunch to his shoulders, unless the flame of his eyes had flared more brightly. He said, between his teeth: "Go ahead."

"This man called me and told me that," Simpson stammered on. "Then he hung up. Several days later he called again, and I was half crazy with fear by then. He said he would send me some money and that with it I was to buy stock in the Bessmo Corporation, that I was to pyramid the earnings until further orders." Simpson licked his lips; his eyes slid sideways to the clock and his words spilled out faster than ever. "I did that, thinking I was getting off easy. A while later, he told me to rent a safety-deposit box, put the shares in that and then to convert all dividends into cash and place that in the box, too. I did that, too, and thought that at last I had a way to find out who held the papers. The bank wouldn't tell me who shared my box, had orders not to. I... I intended either to buy him off, or... or...."

159

"Kill him," the Spider supplied.

Simpson's stare at the gun was like the fascinated stare of a snake-charmed bird. "I hid and watched at the bank where I had rented the box and didn't see anyone. But the next night two men came to my house and beat me up terribly. I was in the hospital for ten days."

"But you went again?"

"I went again," Simpson admitted. "I had to, you see. I couldn't go on not knowing when the blow would fall, when the roof would be snatched from over the heads of my wife and daughter, when my disgrace would strike them down. I went again and saw a man I knew was a minor stockholder in Bessmo enter the bank vaults. Later, when I went to the box I shared with this blackmailer whom the bank was protecting, I found the money gone, found a note telling me to put no more money in the box and that later I would be told what to do with it. By this time the buildings were beginning to fall and I became terribly afraid. I... I felt that there was a connection, a reason why this man did not want his stock in Bessmo listed in his own name, and this seemed to explain it. I knew that Bessmo would resist whatever was causing buildings to collapse. I was afraid."

"This small stockholder," Wentworth said, and hesitated, his voice choking. He felt that he was on the brink of a discovery that would solve the whole case, that would bring to book the man behind all these killings and crashes, the Master himself. His heart thudded in his throat "This small stockholder you saw entering the bank. He was... Alrecht?"

Simpson shivered. "You know everything," he said faintly. "It was Alrecht."

CHAPTER 16
BRIGGS, THE HERO

THE SPIDER flung back his head and laughed. It was derisive, self-mockery. Alrecht, of course, but Alrecht had disappeared. He was a will-o'-the wisp, a shadow in the darkness. Simpson was babbling words, eyes darting from the gun to the clock which stood now at one minute past two.

"It's the truth," he was stammering. *"For God's sake, Spider, believe me!"*

Wentworth ceased his flat laughter. "I do," he said. "You deserve death for that other crime you committed, for the deaths of half a hundred school children, but you can purchase your way out of that. I want the key to the safety-deposit box, and I want your absolute silence about what has happened tonight. If you so much as breathe a word of it, I will know, and I will come for you. And next time, there will be nothing you can say to stave off my avenging bullet."

Simpson stammered in fear. The key, he said, had been stolen from him. Throughout the long drive back to his home he kept that up. Finally Wentworth was convinced he spoke the truth and the man sputtered his gratitude that he was allowed to live. Wentworth was confident now that he had a clue to the Master.

But the next day's investigation was a disappointment. The name on the bank's register card for the man who shared Simpson's safety deposit vault was "John Smith" and the man who had been accustomed to recognize the holders of boxes and admit them to the vaults could not describe "Smith." He was dead—had been crushed to death in the fall of a building two days before.

Signatures of Alrecht were not obtainable for comparison. His bachelor quarters were clean of any handwriting. His bank, the First National in Middleton, had been destroyed. Such friends as could be found had no letters, though one said vaguely that a Photostat of the John Smith signature seemed familiar.

Nita and the others had set sail for New York on the *Britannia* and were due to arrive in two days. Wentworth, seated in Kirkpatrick's office, watched the reports come across the Commissioner's desk. They were like men in war time, these two.

When the carroty-haired cop who kept watch outside the Commissioner's door thrust in an excited head, both men looked up at him with a curious expectant tension.

"Eddie Blanton, of the *Press*," said carrot-top, and the two settled back into their seats wearily. Kirkpatrick raised an indifferent hand in consent of the man's admittance and Blanton came in briskly. Wentworth eyed him intently. Brisk movement in Blanton was a signal of excitement. Usually he lounged, a cigarette dangling from his mouth, the slouch gray hat on at any angle, the baggy topcoat soggy about his ankles. But now the coat swung out behind him, slapping quick-moving calves.

"Listen, Kirk," he said swiftly. "We got a hot tip on the *Britannia,* and the chief didn't even want me to talk to you over the phone about it."

162

Wentworth felt a slow, cold tension stiffen his back. He dropped the report he was scanning on his knees and his gray-blue eyes fixed on Blanton. There was a grin on the reporter's face and a tightness about his eyes that meant big news. But big news to him might mean disaster....

"What about the *Britannia?*" Kirkpatrick's voice was hard and quick.

"Is she or isn't she carrying five millions in gold?" Blanton demanded.

Wentworth's fears—eased. He still sat rigidly, eyeing Blanton.

Kirkpatrick frowned. "I can't say anything for publication on that, Eddie," he said slowly.

"Can you tell me whether you're planning a heavy police guard at the dock?"

"Don't start that business," Kirkpatrick growled. "You're not going to worm a damned thing out of me, and you know it."

Wentworth was leaning forward now. "I've got some friends on the *Britannia*, Blanton," he said slowly. "Somebody who could give you some good detail stuff."

Blanton spun toward him, shrewd brown eyes gleaming. "Where'd you get the tip from?" he demanded.

Wentworth was on his feet in an instant. "I thought so, damn it," he said. "Out with it, Blanton. What's happened on the *Britannia?*"

Kirkpatrick stared from one man to the other, leaning back in his chair. "What's this all about?"

BLANTON GRIMACED. "Your friend, Wentworth, just tricked me," he said. "I guess I might as well spill it but keep it under your hat until we can hit the street with an extra. I was really sent over to find out whether anybody else was in on it." He leaned over and picked up Kirkpatrick's phone. "Outside, darling," he told the man operator downstairs, dialed his paper and got hold of the city editor. "All clear, Gibby," he reported. "Naw, not a thing." He hung up.

"Yeah, you tricked me," Blanton told Wentworth, "but just the same I'm going to cash in on that promise of yours."

"Talk, damn you!" Kirkpatrick growled.

Blanton lipped another cigarette, held a burning match and looked over it. "The steel bunch tried to hijack the *Britannia*," he said casually, sucked the flame against the cigarette and blew the match out with smoke. "And dear little Briggsy, none other than our own W. Johnson Briggs, sank 'em with their own stuff."

"What!" Amazement showed on Wentworth's face.

"Uh-huh, that's just the way I feel," said Blanton, grinning. He told them with the concise efficiency of a man used to handling big news what had happened aboard the *Britannia*. A fast yacht had hailed the big British steamer in the midst of an Atlantic storm and ordered it to lay to and surrender its five million in gold. If the captain refused, the yacht's message read, the *Britannia* would be subjected to a whiff of gas that would make her steel plates break to pieces. In other words, the yacht would loose a load of the steel-eater and sink the *Britannia* without a trace.

Wentworth's fists were knotted at his side. He could see the picture that Blanton threw before them so vividly, the two ships heaving on the gale-swept Atlantic, giant and pigmy, and the giant at the mercy of the smaller boat. Stricken with the steel-eater, her plates would not hold together a minute in these waves. Instant dissolution. Two thousand persons plunged into wild waters from which there could be no rescue....

"Little Briggsy romped up to the captain," Blanton went on. "The news had leaked out somehow. 'Listen, cap,' he says. 'If we can make even a mild sort of demolition bomb we can beat them off.'"

The captain had heeded Briggs. While they stalled and parleyed with the yacht, powder from pistol bullets was rigged up into a weak bomb, the plane that hopped ashore with the mail from twelve hours at sea was hitched to the catapult and the pilot took off. At the same time the *Britannia* spun about and headed to windward of the yacht. There was a big yell from the yacht, then the mail pilot swooped over it and dropped his bomb. It was weak, so he didn't have to worry about being blown up while flying too close. He split a gas tank on the deck just as Briggs had recommended, and before he had got a hundred yards away, the yacht went to pieces.

"They got the full dose of their own gas," Blanton said. "The ship just broke up in pieces. Now, Mr. Wentworth, I've told all. How about putting me in touch with that somebody on the *Britannia?*"

Wentworth found that he had been standing so stiffly his muscles ached with the strain of it. He lifted a hand and plunked a fist against a palm. "That was splendidly done, by God," he said.

"How about that phone call to the *Britannia*, Wentworth?" Blanton insisted.

Wentworth nodded, crossed to the desk. He picked up the phone.

"Commissioner," a voice said rapidly. "I was just calling. Here's something the cop on the beat thinks you ought to hear about. A man was found burned with acid near the Funsdall National Bank. He was in an auto and...."

WENTWORTH SAID, "Wait a minute," turned to Kirkpatrick and repeated what he had been told. His eyes narrowed suddenly, his fist struck the desk. "By Heaven, Kirk," he said. "They're going to attack the Funsdall National with the steel-eater!"

Blanton spun and his coat flapped out from him. He went toward the door in a fast dive. Wentworth reached him in two long strides, caught him by the shoulder. The reporter came about with his fist swinging, but it skidded off Wentworth's forearm and he found himself held helpless.

"Not yet, Blanton," Wentworth said quietly. "This is the first chance we've had to be on the scene before they struck and you're not going to warn them off with your paper."

Behind them, Kirkpatrick was clipping out orders over the telephone with the rapid efficiency for organization that made him the most successful police commissioner New York had ever had. Blanton wriggled his shoulders, sighed and subsided.

Kirkpatrick heel-pounded across the office, and Wentworth pulled Blanton along with them. They entered Kirkpatrick's big sedan, and the driver whirled it on a dime and sent them roaring downtown.

Above the roaring din of the powerful motor, there came

another more ominous sound. The scattered banging of pistols and the chattering fury of machine guns!

New power droned into the engine. The sedan leaped and quivered with the force, lunged forward with mounting speed. The siren began to moan, its note rising, swelling until its shriek burst through the streets in terrific volume. Wentworth coolly took his two guns from their holsters. He knew they were in perfect condition, but it was comfortable to feel their weight. He clicked back the bolt, saw the gleam of brass in each chamber and thrust the automatics back into their holster clips. He was conscious of Blanton's eyes upon him. The reporter's face was pale and he had a deprecating grin on his mouth.

"Gun noise always makes me nervous," he apologized.

Wentworth laughed sharply. He was excited. He had more in mind than merely battling these gangsters who would be looting the Funsdall Bank. For days he had been seeking a new contact with the Master and always it eluded him. He could not even discover through which mob he worked now. This was a new chance. Out of the moil of battle just ahead, victory might come, and a clue to Baldy. Wentworth was thinking warmly of Briggs. The dapper, animated little architect had played a game part. He owed Nita's life to him, he realized, for it was obvious that the pirates had intended to destroy the *Britannia* and all aboard once they had the loot under their own hatches.

HIS THOUGHTS cut off and he braced himself with feet and thighs as the sedan skidded around a corner, straightened with its rear swinging, and swooped up a narrow cross-street between the cliffs of skyscrapers. There were gapes here and there in the rows, shattered windows presented blank eyes and the sedan dodged pits in the street. Once more a whipping turn, this time to the left, and a khaki of National Guardsmen showed. The brakes snagged and rubber whined; the sedan's rear seemed to rise with the suddenness of the stop. It slewed sidewise and Wentworth went out first, guns in his hands. Kirkpatrick was right behind him. A blue uniformed police officer, a lieutenant, puffed up at a run.

"They're inside the bank, sir," he panted. "Wiped out every man in sight with machine guns before they went in."

The proof of his statement lay in the streets, scattered bodies in brown and blue. But the robbers were trapped. Behind barricades of autos, the khaki troops, reinforced by police, waited with leveled rifles, with ready machine guns. Wentworth ran an alert eye over the defenses, heard the lieutenant report that the bank was surrounded in just this way. Then a machine gun opened up from a window.

A soldier twenty yards away tilted up the muzzle of a Lewis gun, shoulders hunched to take its recoil, and squeezed on the trigger. The gun exploded in his hands. The bolt ripped through the side of his face, hurled him kicking to the ground. His helper, standing ready with a drum of ammunition, stared stupidly and a blast from the machine gun in the bank's window smashed his head to bits.

Kirkpatrick cursed viciously, strode toward the lines, and a whistle shrilled. Soldiers threw up their rifles, aiming at that window of death. What was intended as a volley turned into a mass suicide. Every rifle of the twenty aimed at that window exploded in the hands of the soldiers.

Wentworth stared down at the automatic in his hand with twisted lips, then he plunged forward also.

"Cease firing!" he shouted, and his cry was a mockery. There's wasn't a soldier at this barricade except the white-faced sergeant who had trilled the whistle. He, too, was staring stupidly at the automatic he held in his hand. Wentworth seized his arm.

"Where's the commanding officer?" he snapped.

The sergeant gestured toward a cigar store at the side of the street whose windows had long since been smashed by lead. Wentworth plunged toward it at a dead run, saw cement dust kick up in his path and wrenched aside, dived to the cover of the automobile barricade. Bullets drummed fiercely against it.

When firing stopped, he jumped to his feet, reached the store at a dead run, found the major in charge.

"They've turned the steel-eater loose on the guns," Wentworth barked. "They'll all explode. The bayonet is our only chance. They'll have to be used carefully or they'll crumble."

The Major stared at him a moment, then caught the drift of the words.

"You're Major Wentworth," he nodded. "I was in your company once, over there. Give me a hand, will you? I've lost three officers, and…."

Wentworth cut him short with a jerk of his hand. "Couriers to order cease firing," he barked. "With your permission, Major, I'll organize a bayonet squad." His mouth twisted thinly. "I always had a theory I taught my own sergeants that two inches

169

of the bayonet was plenty to kill. It will have to be today, and the thrusts will all have to be in the guts. Those blades, weakened by the steel eater, won't stand even a throat job today."

The major assented with a crisp nod, jerked off hat and coat and flung them at Wentworth. "That will give you authority," he said.

Wentworth hauled himself into the coat while machine guns drummed on. But the soldiers were not shooting now. The couriers had reached them with orders not to fire. Wentworth reached the side-door of the store in a stride, dived out and rolled to the cover of a barricade. Men in khaki were crouched there white-faced. They were not regular army men, just boys who loved military atmosphere and had signed up with the national guard. A few of their officers had seen overseas service; none of the boys had. They were clenching their bayoneted rifles but they had no confidence in them. They had ceased to be weapons for defense and attack and had become dangerous to the men who held them.

"Men," Wentworth pitched his voice above the chatter of the gangster guns, "Your guns cannot be fired, but your bayonets are still good, if you use them right." Eyes turned to him, showed doubt at his strangely mixed garb. But his voice commanded obedience, his manner carried authority. "You need only two inches of the blade," Wentworth hammered on, "and that means two inches only. That will kill, will knock a man out cold on his feet the moment you pull the steel out of him. But remember, two inches only, and that here." He jabbed a finger into his abdomen below the parting of his ribs. "Right there and nowhere else!"

CHAPTER 17
THE SPIDER WAGES BATTLE!

H E WHIRLED, plucked a rifle from a soldier beside him and gripped it with light and ready hands. "These men we are going against have killed thousands," he said, "but they are cowards. They have killed by pushing buildings down on innocent men and women. We are the first who have had a chance to even that score." He looked about him and saw grimness creeping into the faces of these boys, saw their hands tensing on their rifles. "Remember, two inches of steel *in the guts!*" He paused, drew a deep breath. *"Follow me!"*

With the word, he sprang to the hood of an automobile, vaulted clear and charged toward the bank. He had chosen his point of attack well. He was out of range of the window where the machine gun stammered, out of the line of the door. Yells rang out from all sides. An excited policeman leaped to the top of an automobile and threw down on the window with a submachine gun. It blasted to pieces in his hands, blew his stomach in so that he doubled over the shattered weapon. The ludicrous surprise on his face was instantly erased by the sponge of death.

Wentworth swung around the corner and a gangster with a machine gun at his hip gaped at him. He lifted the muzzle and Wentworth's rifle thrust out as lightly as a foil. The bayonet slid in over the machine gun, prodded through the man's clothing

171

and was whipped out. The man's eyes closed and he slumped down. Blood welled out and spread over the steps in a widening pool.

Wentworth was flat against the wall behind one of the

The twenty-ton truck rammed the gangster car—ground over the wreckage!

polished columns now, soldiers behind him and opposite him behind the other column.

The glass of the doors smashed to the stone floor and two soldiers against the opposite wall pitched to the steps across their guns. One bayonet struck point-on and shattered. Inside, a machine gun racketed. The hallway was a sounding chamber. The blasts were thunderous.

Wentworth turned his head. "Grenade," he said crisply.

A heavy rough piece of iron was thrust into his hand. Wentworth yanked the pin and tossed the bomb through the shattered doors. The grenade's blast was oddly muffled and Wentworth nodded. The steel-eater had weakened the casing so that the force of the explosion was greatly reduced, but it still should do heavy damage. The machine gun had stopped. Wentworth sprang toward the doors.

There were cheers behind him now, cheers of men who saw hope for the first time. They went through the glassless doors in a resolute swift wave, bayonets thrusting ahead. They penetrated the inner door and a close group of men wheeled from a bank entrance on their left. Wentworth sprang close, his bayonet point snaking out. A man flung up his hands and went down screaming. Wentworth reached past him as he fell, but he could not get at the stomach of the next gangster and the man's pistol was coming up. He ran him through the throat and the steel snapped off short.

WENTWORTH HAD no time to snatch a fallen gun, no time even to think. There were five gangsters left. A pistol blasted and a soldier screamed. Falling, his head struck Wentworth's calves. He sagged slightly, pitched forward with the butt of his rifle sweeping upward. It crunched into the groin of another gangster and the man squealed, doubled over. The butt swept on, the rifle coming up over Wentworth's shoulder, and he grabbed it, thrust forward with all his weight behind the butt. It smashed a man's face.

On his right, a soldier ran his bayonet its full length into another gangster's stomach. A man behind the hood fired almost in the trooper's face and even as his bloodied head jerked back between his shoulder blades, a companion's bayonet slipped into the throat of the gangster. The hallway was cleared for the moment.

"Take their pistols," he barked over his shoulder, and stooped to scoop up two himself. There were only four soldiers behind him now. They were white-faced and alert. He nodded encouragement and slipped into the lobby of the bank. There were bodies scattered over the floor, steel cashier's cages were smashed and the vault-door was wrecked, but there was not a gangster in sight. Wentworth and his shattered squad raced the length of the long room, spotted an open door on the side and darted toward it.

Wentworth checked for a moment in that doorway, his face gone gray. Death confronted him. Death in a half-hundred scattered corpses of blue and khaki. He plunged on, darting toward the auto barricade. He lifted the body of a policeman from the fender of one of the cars, flung himself into the driver's seat and kicked the starter.

"Get five rifles with bayonets," he ordered.

He was frowning heavily as he flung the car about, as the four men who remained piled in. In some way, the gangsters had rendered their own guns immune to the gas. Either that, or the steel-eater had hovered so close to the ground that by raising themselves to the height of the bank's floor, they had been above the level that would affect guns. What wind there had been had blown from the East, and if the gas had been released so as to affect all the troops and police about the bank, it would have had to affect their own weapons, too.

Wentworth sent the car hurtling ahead, swung around a corner. Blocks away he could hear the shriek of sirens that betokened the chase. He flung on in pursuit, forehead still corrugated in thought.

Up ahead, the gangsters would run into police whose weapons had not been weakened by the gas, but slamming along in force as they were, no ordinary squad would have strength enough to stop them. Wentworth spun another corner and yanked violently at the wheel, barely skating aside from the wreckage of a police auto. In his one swift glance, he saw that the wheels of the police car had gone to pieces, all four of them. His lips shut grimly. A new use for the steel-eater. The gangsters had trailed it behind them in their flight and it had wrecked the car of at least one pursuer.

Wentworth flung a look ahead, saw two more cars piled up. He nodded his head. It was clever strategy, but there was a way to beat it. Three blocks to the right of the line of chase Wentworth hurled his car, then paralleled it with the motor roaring wide open. The robbers' defense had a defect. If they were to protect themselves by the gas, the gangsters must flee in a straight line. Otherwise, they might well double back upon their own weapon and be defeated by it. Police probably would not realize the reason for their cars crashing until too late to profit by the knowledge.

The accelerator was pinned to the floor and Wentworth's car rocketed along at close to seventy. He jammed the horn in place with a pin and with it blaring for right of way as he raced on. Traffic was already disrupted by the wails of sirens. It dodged aside, gave Wentworth and his four soldiers a clear path. It was possible to keep track of the chase by the sirens and the scattering bursts of shots from the gangster cars. Gradually those sounds came nearer and finally dropped behind and still Wentworth crushed the accelerator to the floor and burned the street northward.

FINALLY HE swung left once more, toward the line of escape. His mind was racing with the swift roar of his engine. It would be a futile thing to dash these five lives into the path of the gangsters. Something more was needed than five automatics, for which they had no extra ammunition.

His car crossed Fourth Avenue in a bound and he stood on the brakes, jerked his head toward the-soldiers on the rear seat.

"You and you," he picked two with his eyes, "commandeer trucks and block Fifth Avenue."

The two men sprang out instantly with their rifles and Wentworth sent his machine lurching on, crossed Fifth Avenue and hurtled Broadway, where he ordered the last two soldiers to block the street with cars and trucks. Then he raced on, circled two blocks back along the line of chase and found an interurban truck lumbering southward with a heavy trailer behind. Wentworth stopped it, flung to the driver's seat, rifle in hand.

"Out," he barked. "I'm taking the truck for police business."

The men stared at his haphazard uniform, started to argue and decided not to as Wentworth clambered up with the business end of the bayonet forward. The truckmen dropped off and he started the truck with a lurch, headed east toward Broadway. The sirens and shots were racing nearer. Then the siren stopped and Wentworth guessed that the last of the police cars had gone to pieces under the assault of the steel eater. He crouched low behind the steel front of the truck and waited, saw six cars sweep up Broadway in a close bunch. Then he started the truck lurching forward again, turned into their wake.

He heard the frantic squeal of brakes, and grim laughter bubbled up from his chest. Two trucks, traveling abreast, had swung out into Broadway and were trundling straight toward the gangster cars. A blasting fury of gun shots ripped out from the mob cars and one of the trucks swerved, locked wheels with the other and turned them both over in a splintering wreck upon the street. They blocked it from curb to curb, slopped up on the sidewalks. There was no escape for the gangster cars. The leader had almost rammed into the wrecked trucks. Now he began to back and whirl southward again.

Wentworth had reached the corner of the block in which they were trapped. He angled his huge truck and trailer across the street, set the truck running wild toward the gangster cars and dropped from the driver's seat. He had two guns and the rifle and he flung himself flat on the street and began firing beneath the body of his truck. The huge twenty-tonner wheeled on. The leading gangster's car halted and men scattered from it. An instant later the nose of the truck rammed the car, ground over the wreckage. From the debris, a faint, almost imperceptible gas filtered upward, then settled heavily toward the street. The street was completely blocked and gangsters scattered from the other cars also. A machine gun stuttered and bullets began to pock the asphalt beneath the truck. Suddenly, the machine gun stopped. It stopped with a blasting explosion that hurled its wielder bloodily to the ground. An automatic exploded in another man's hand and Wentworth laughed grimly as he pumped out his last bullets. The steel-eater had turned on its users. Their own guns were crippled now.

With a yell, he bounded to his feet, snatching up the bayoneted rifle which he had carried with him. His shout brought one soldier from the wreckage of the trucks and around the corner from Fifth Avenue two others pounded. In the hands of each, a bayoneted rifle was gripped. More than one of those bayonets was tipped with red.

"Their guns are useless, men!" Wentworth yelled. "Remember, two inches of steel in the guts!"

He hurtled forward at a dead run, his bayoneted gun at port across his body. Two more gangsters tried in their excitement to shoot and the weapons blew up and tore their hands with their explosions. The bolt smashed one man's face, then the whole group turned and ran. Thirty men, turned and ran frenziedly from four. But they were weaponless, their morale had been shattered when their sure defense turned upon them and stripped them of guns. And the four attackers had long knives that would stab, two inches deep, into their guts. The underworld murderers turned and fled.

A SOLDIER overtook Wentworth and the Spider snatched another grenade from the man, hurled it toward the fleeing gangsters. It smashed with the same oddly muffled blast, but flying fragments felled two men. The other soldier, charging from the opposite end of the block, snatched out a grenade and hurled it. Another gangster spun on his heels and went down. Then the leaders reached a subway kiosk.

"Down here!" one hood yelled. "They can't throw grenades down here!"

The gangsters funneled into the subway, rats scampering to cover. Wentworth caught a grenade from a soldier and whirled toward the kiosk on the opposite side of the street. Where the gangsters had entered, they could reach only downtown trains, trains that would shoot them back into the arms of the police from whom they fled. But by climbing down and crossing the tracks, they could catch an uptown train. That was what Wentworth raced to prevent.

He darted down the stairs, sprang to the uptown platform as the gangsters streamed out on the opposite side. Wentworth trailed his bayoneted rifle in his left hand. In his right, he held the grenade. The leading gangster, plunging for the tracks, reeled back and his companions collided with him. Wentworth cursed viciously. The leader was McSwag! Somehow he had gathered a fresh mob and returned to the assault. The red Spider glimmered on his forehead and Wentworth had sworn to put a bullet on that spot the next time they met, yet he was helpless without arms… He raised the grenade.

"Surrender," he shouted, "or I'll blow the roof down on all of you."

McSwag's lips writhed, but what he said was drowned in the thunder of an approaching train. It was on the downtown side and it slid its steel sides between Wentworth and his prey. The gangsters streamed in as the doors opened and through the windows. Wentworth saw the three soldiers charging toward the turnstiles with bayonets ready. He saw McSwag race toward the front car, knock the conductor aside and press the buttons that controlled the slide doors, operated by compressed air. The doors slid shut. The motorman, unaware that anything untoward had occurred, got the electric flash of the automatic signal indicating the doors were shut and the train slid forward. The soldiers hammered against the doors, too late. As the train gathered headway, Wentworth saw McSwag striding toward the motorman's cubicle in the first car.

He cursed, but lowered the grenade. There were a hundred innocent persons aboard that train. He could not wreck it, even to wipe out this gang of murders. He felt the platform beneath him shaking to the vibration of the departing train, and suddenly his eyes flew wide. He swung about and slapped through the exit doors from the platform, yanked open the door of the station-agent's booth.

"Stop all trains," he shouted hoarsely.

The station agent gaped at him.

"Stop the trains, fool," Wentworth snarled at him. "The steel-eater has been spread all along the streets above the subway. The gas is heavy and will settle into the tubes; the vibration…."

He choked, reeled, caught the side of the door and stood trembling while a rumbling, hollow concussion roared through the tunnel. The lights blinked out and for a moment, utter silence followed the echoes of the cave-in.

"Too late," Wentworth said hoarsely. "Too late!" He pushed himself away from the doors of the booth, made his way heavily up the steps to daylight. The soldiers boiled out of the opposite exit, stared down the street. Four blocks down Broadway, the pavement had dropped through. Thereafter, for five blocks, the street had become a great crater. The roof of the subway had fallen in.

The gangsters had carried another hundred persons with them to death, but it was a cosmic retribution that had been visited upon them.

The weapon that they had used against others had crushed them in turn!

CHAPTER 18
TWO THOUSAND SHALL DIE!

WENTWORTH STOOD in the ruined street in his parti-uniform dress and rocked his knuckles across his forehead while the soldiers stood by with their bloody bayonets. McSwag! His presence here, his leadership of this new mob meant something, Wentworth knew, but what was it? The meaning was vital; he knew that from the sharp excitement that tingled through his veins.

Abruptly, a hoarse cry sounded in his throat, low and muffled, a hoarse cry that meant discovery and triumph. He broke into a headlong sprint, finally found a taxi. "Police headquarters, *fast!*" he barked.

The taxi driver took him literally, doing a fandango of speed among the pits in the streets, the blocks of roped-off debris. Wentworth sat on the edge of his seat with his fists clenched on his knees, his head thrust alertly forward. His body swayed to the jerks of the bucking cab. His face was white and eager. He knew now where to find the Master—not who he was, but where to find him! There would be around two thousand other persons at the same place, but there was a way to pick him out!

The Spider and the police had burned down gang after gang, only to have the terror of the Master rise phoenix-like from the ashes. Once more that feat would be performed, once more death and destruction would be scattered broadcast over the land. The Master was insatiable. There would be no end of peril until he died. Wentworth flung from the cab, tossing money at the driver, and went up the steps of the Centre Street station in giant bounds. The Master should die!

Wentworth punched open the door into Kirkpatrick's sanctum without announcement, sprang to the telephone and got hold of the hangar where his seaplane was kept.

"Bring it to the Battery dock at once," he ordered. "What the hell has rough water got to do with it? At once, I said!"

He slammed up, got hold of Professor Brownlee. "My weapon, is it ready?"

He nodded in satisfaction at the news that a courier was on the way with it, ordered a radio phone call for Nita on the *Britannia*, then, straightened, barking words at the staring Kirkpatrick.

"The Master is abroad the *Britannia!*" he snapped. "I'm flying out. There'll be room for you if you want to go."

"If I want to?" Kirkpatrick was on his feet at once, striding to the wardrobe in the corner. "The murderer is still at work. An elevated train went through its tracks a half hour ago and killed more than twenty people."

Not curses, but savage laughter rose to Wentworth's lips. *"He shall pay!"* He went out the door with pounding heels and Kirkpatrick crowded behind him. His heavy sedan rocketed southward through the streets, passing rows of hearses and ambulances carrying the dead and injured from the scenes of the Master's latest atrocities, past the strewn bodies where the soldiers had fallen, past the cavern where the subway victims lay dead. But all that was a blurred picture of speed.

"How do you know the Master is on the *Britannia?*" Kirkpatrick demanded as the two of them swayed jerkily to the howling speed of the car.

"McSwag was the leader of the bank mob," Wentworth told him, his eyes fixed ahead, subconsciously picking the path for the car through the traffic. He nodded, turned his head. "Your driver is almost as good as my Jackson," he said.

Kirkpatrick swore. "What the hell has McSwag leading that mob got to do with the Master being on the *Britannia*?"

"It means that since the Spider wiped out McSwag's mob in Brooklyn, the night the bridge fell, Baldy has made no fresh contact with the gangsters." There was a curious smile on Wentworth's mouth. "If you will recall, none of your stoolies, nor all your police have been able to catch so much as a hint of Baldy being seen—Baldy is a conspicuous figure with his bald head and his cast eye!"

"But Baldy and the Master are two different men," said Kirkpatrick doggedly, "and I'd like to know before I risk my life in this crazy flight just what is behind your deductions."

THE SEDAN braked roughly to a halt, its locked rear wheels dribbling over the concrete. Wentworth flung out and slammed into a dock house, grabbed a pay phone. "That call to the *Britannia*?" he demanded. He got the connection, got Nita.

"Darling," he said rapidly, "for the next six or seven hours I want you to become garrulous. I want you to tell everybody that your fiancé is in with the police and that he has found out the Master of the wreckers is abroad the *Britannia*. Also that he has a clue that will identify the Master definitely. You may go even farther, darling, and tell them your fiancé's exact words: that he said he had the 'key to the situation.' Yes, darling, I know you don't know what I'm talking about, but the Master does. And here's something else to do. Have Anse organize the crew, with the captain's help, and keep watch on every American on board. You watch Butterworth yourself. What am I expecting? Why, the key to the situation will show itself. Honest, dearest, it's not a

"If one of you moves," he said, "the ship sinks!" He held the

portfolio raised above his head, a gun in the other hand.

riddle. Not a word to anyone but Anse now, beautiful, or it might leak out to the Master before we're ready. First Anse, sweetheart, then turn gossip. And we'll see you soon. Yes, we're flying out."

Kirkpatrick glared at him. "Damn it, Dick," he said. "I trust you, but I wish you'd tell me what it's all about before I risk my neck in this fool hop."

Wentworth spun to face him. "It's a long chance, Kirk," he said. "A damn' long one, but it may trap the Master. Until we do that, not a man or woman in this country is safe. We beat the gangsters today, but now that the steel-eater has demonstrated its ability to destroy guns, nothing will be immune to attack. They could strip the treasury itself. An enemy equipped with the secret of the steel-eater could sweep us off the earth."

Kirkpatrick agreed, still angry and plucking at his spike-ended mustache in irritation.

Wentworth strode out into the open, set his teeth as the bite of the fresh wind from the seat cut into him, and pushed his heavily-coated body into it until he stood by the stringpiece, staring grim-eyed at a small speck that showed above Governor's Island and winged rapidly toward them. A man strode to him with a package. "From Professor Brownlee, sir."

Wentworth nodded curtly, took the package in both hands. Kirkpatrick stood beside him with his fists rammed into his pockets. "All right," he said. "McSwag is the key. Now what?" He had to raise his voice to make it audible above the whip of the wind and the sullen boom of waves against the stone bulkhead.

"It proves," Wentworth said drily, "that the Master has been abroad since McSwag was beaten the first time."

"But how do you know he's aboard the *Britannia?*"

Wentworth's lips twisted stiffly. "Because the *Britannia* was attacked," he said. Kirkpatrick's oath was inarticulate, but he dropped his questioning. He saw that Wentworth did not intend to give the explanation yet and he stared at the seaplane, circling now to a landing on the rough waters.

"He can't make it!" Kirkpatrick muttered, the words sucked from his lips by the wind. But the pilot did make it, and seven hours later, Wentworth duplicated his feat on long sliding billows beside the *Britannia,* kept the plane taxiing there until a hoist boom dropped a hook that lifted them to the decks. He carefully unwrapped the package he had received from Brownlee and thrust the glittering gun it contained in his belt.

The British Captain, dour-faced above a heavy white mustache, was stiffly indignant at this further delay to the *Britannia's* progress, already slowed by storm and the brush with the pirates. Nita and Anse Collins met Wentworth in the captain's private cabin, but to his eager questions they responded only with shakes of their heads.

"I reckon I don't know exactly what's up," Anse Collins said slowly, "but I didn't see a soul throw anything overboard."

Wentworth nodded, keen eyes on the tall deputy's face.

"Alrecht is on board," he said, "but he's in disguise. Nita, I think we'd better hold a council of war in your suite. Anse, get Nancy and Briggs. Ram Singh's already down in the suite. Come on, Kirk."

WENTWORTH STRODE down to C deck where Nita had taken a cabin. His head was up, but inwardly he was worried.

189

He had counted a great deal on trapping the Master by his talk of the "key" to the situation, a reference the Master would have understood meant the key to the safety deposit-box he had shared with O'Leary Simpson. He had hoped the Master would throw it overboard, but the Master had outguessed him, had figured that his feint was precisely that.

At the door of Nita's cabin, Wentworth was halted by a page boy in a neat short-jacketed uniform who proffered a small silver tray on which lay an envelope. Wentworth glanced down from it to the boy's face.

"Where did you get this?" he demanded swiftly.

"It was on the desk when I returned from a call, sir," the boy reported.

Wentworth nodded, thanked him, took the—envelope carefully and slit it open. Within was a single sheet of paper. There was one sentence on it.

If you find me, this ship sinks and two thousand people die.—
THE MASTER.

Wentworth grinned crookedly at the message and passed it over to Kirkpatrick. "Our bluff worked partly," he said. "We at least forced the Master to admit his presence. Do you believe me now?"

Kirkpatrick said quietly, "I always believe you, Dick."

As they entered Nita's suite, Ram Singh rose from beside a bunk where a motionless figure lay. His eyes glinted as they met his master's and he swept a *salaam* almost to the floor. He did not speak. Wentworth glanced only cursorily at the man on the bunk, who, face turned to the wall, seemed utterly indifferent to the visitors, but Kirkpatrick crossed and stared down at him. There was a tap at the door and Nancy came in with Briggs and Anse behind her. Briggs was carrying a thick portfolio of leather, puffing a black cigar. "Can't get away from my work," he spluttered. "Carrying it with me. Figuring on a new skyscraper. Take place of Sky Building."

Wentworth clasped his hand warmly. "That was splendid work you did wiping out that ship load of pirates."

Brigg's curiously contradictory face with its keen eyes above van Dyke and imperial wrinkled with good humor. "Did a bit of killing on your own what I hear."

Wentworth smiled, amazed that Briggs had been so interested in his activities. He waited until the small talk stopped, until the people in the room were watching him seriously.

"The Master is aboard," he said, and watched the smiles wash themselves off the faces of Briggs and Nancy, saw Anse Collins' sharp blue eyes flicker and chill. "He says that if I find him, he will destroy the ship."

Briggs puffed excitedly on his cigar. "Must find him," he barked out, his voice going loud. "Find the steel-eater gas."

"Quite so," agreed Kirkpatrick. "But how? Remember, if we fumble at all, we and two thousand others die."

WENTWORTH WAS standing erect, his hands idle at his sides, his head thrust forward aggressively. "We are not without a clue," he said briskly. "I had deduced that the Master was abroad, and other deductions led to that. His presence on this ship confirms them all. The Master was a cautious man.

191

He covered every step of his work, protected himself behind a dozen shields." Wentworth described swiftly how he had got his money through O'Leary Simpson, how he spoke always through a mouthpiece whom he never saw personally.

"When a mob became too powerful for him to handle," Wentworth went on, "he dropped a clue to police or to the Spider and had it destroyed."

He paused, looked swiftly about the faces in the room. There was keen interest on the faces of the men. Nita was calmly confident, a slight smile on her full red lips, her blue eyes on his. Nancy Collins was frightened. She alone of those in the room seemed to sense the peril that overhung them... *If you find me, the ship will sink...* Wentworth knew that was no idle threat, knew that the Master was fully capable of fulfilling his threat, knew that he would have means at hand. He need only release his steel-eater, and not all the labor of the entire crew could save the *Britannia* from plunging downward through the black waters, her hull shattered fragments of gray powder that had been steel.

He turned toward Kirkpatrick, "Kirk, I had a talk with Beatrice Ross. She was thoroughly chastened after her imprisonment. But more than that, she was eager to get back at the Spider. She told me about his crashing in on McSwag's hideout that night. She said that the way Baldy proved his identity to the gangsters when the Spider came there in Baldy's disguise, was to have one of the gangsters *feel his bald head!*"

Kirkpatrick's hard blue eyes were upon him. Anse Collins was breathing heavily through his mouth and Briggs' cigar had gone out again. Wentworth met Nita's eyes and shook his head slightly.

"Baldy really was bald. Otherwise, the fact that the Spider's apparently bald head was false would not have been a factor in determining which was the real Baldy.

"The Master never did a thing when he could get some one else to perform for him… that is if there was personal danger involved," Wentworth continued. "He tipped off McSwag's raid on the Funsdall bank!"

"The hell he did!" This from Kirkpatrick.

"Remember, an acid-burned body was found near the bank?" Wentworth asked. "That was the tip-off. The day before that, he had revealed through the attack on the *Britannia* that the weapon used was acid gas!"

Kirkpatrick's blue eyes were dubious. "But the *Britannia* might well have been destroyed without a trace, without a survivor to tell of the acid gas."

Wentworth shook his head slowly. "No Kirk," he said softly. "I think that if Briggs had not supplied the way out, the thing would have been accomplished in another way. I think the Master intended the destruction of the yacht and all aboard, just as he contrived McSwag's downfall. But these are minor points; what I am pointing out is the caution of the man. Invariably, he used *some one else* to destroy the hirelings for whom he no longer had any use." He paused and drew a deep breath, looked again over the six whose eyes were riveted to his face. "The Master was so cautious that I think there is one time when he did not use anyone else, one time when it would have been more dangerous to use some one else than to do the thing himself. I do not believe he trusted any man sufficiently to use him as a mouth-piece, even though all communications were supposed to be by telephone. Baldy has not been spotted in New York despite a most intensive search since the night the McSwag mob was wiped out by the Spider and Betty Briggs was freed." He smiled tightly at Nita. "An hour after you sailed, my dear."

Kirkpatrick broke in sharply. "Hell, you mean...."

Wentworth nodded. "That the Master and Baldy are one and the same man!"

There was startled silence.

"Alrecht may be bald for all we know," said Wentworth quietly.

He stepped quickly to the motionless figure on the bunk, whipped aside the covers and bent over the man.

"Are you bald, Alrecht?" he asked.

"Alrecht!" Kirkpatrick exploded the word, sprang to the bunk and stared down at the prisoner. "But you said you were bringing Butterworth back from England!"

Wentworth nodded. "Quite," he admitted. "But you will remember that this Butterworth never visited his people in Kent, that he made deposits in Alrecht's name, that all trace of Alrecht vanished when Butterworth left the country."

"You mean Butterworth and Alrecht are the same man, too?" Kirkpatrick was incredulous.

"No," Wentworth was smiling thinly down at the indignant face of the lawyer, across whose mouth were strips of gaging adhesive tape. "I only mean that Alrecht went abroad on Butterworth's passport after the picture on it was altered for him. I mean that Butterworth is undoubtedly dead and I suspect that it was his body, burned by acid to prevent identification, that was found beside the Funsdall bank. The Master ordered his elimination, undoubtedly ordered from abroad, to betray McSwag."

Wentworth leaned over and stripped off the adhesive and Alrecht immediately began to splutter out indignant words that sounded rusty. Wentworth caught his hair in both fists and yanked vigorously. The hair did not come loose and Alrecht howled with pain.

"I didn't think he could be the Master," Wentworth said quietly. "But he knows who the Master is. The Master was blackmailing him, probably had his evidence placed somewhere ready to be released in case of his death. That would protect him. The Master was a coward."

"Alrecht knows who the Master is?" asked Kirkpatrick softly. He was standing directly over the bunk and slowly he took off his belt, fingered the buckle. "There should be a way of making Alrecht talk."

CHAPTER 19
THE END OF
THE MURDER MASTER

WENTWORTH TURNED carelessly away from where Alrecht lay, glaring up at Kirkpatrick. He nodded slightly to Nita. It was more a movement of the eyes than of the head. At the same moment, he barked staccato Hindustani words at Ram Singh. The Hindu took two swift strides across the room and seized Briggs' arms. Nita stepped up behind him and, wrapping her fingers in his long hair, yanked fiercely at it. There was a moment of struggle, of panted curses, then the hair came free and revealed an egg-shaped bald head.

Wentworth's gun was in his hand. "W. Johnson Briggs," he said sharply, "you are Baldy. *You are the Master!* There is other damning evidence against you, too. We will find, I think, that you left the *Berengaria* before she sailed, then overtook her by fast boat while she went down the bay. You had to see McSwag once more before you sailed."

"He did do that!" Nancy Briggs cried out. "He said it was business."

"Also," Wentworth said. "I am sure that Alrecht will now confirm that he saw you open the box in which O'Leary Simpson placed Bessmo money."

"He did," said Alrecht grudgingly from the bed. "But I didn't know what it meant I only knew he was afraid when I recognized him."

Wentworth was grinning tensely, eyes watching Briggs with keen attention. "There were two other circumstances which pointed to you, Briggs," he said. "From the description by Ram Singh of Baldy, he smoked a cigarette like a man used to cigars, that is, Baldy wet the entire end of the cigarette with his lips. And you smoke cigars, Briggs.

"Furthermore, the man who got something on the contractor O'Leary Simpson, who got his secret specifications and held them over him to force his cooperation in buying Bessmo stock, must necessarily have been someone connected with the building trade. And you were, Briggs. Then there was the matter of Baldy's big head, and your own as evidenced by that picture of your daughter wearing your hat."

"This is all utter nonsense," Briggs protested hoarsely. "How could I possibly profit from all these murders?"

"That's the simplest part of it," Wentworth told him curtly, "and the fiendish part of it, too. First you got a cut of all the money seized by the criminals with the use of this gas steel-eater that you stole from Jim Collins. Second, you profit from contracts for the rebuilding of skyscrapers, for you are a leading architect of such buildings. Third, you would take in millions through dividends from the Bessmo Corporation, whose stock you held through O'Leary Simpson. Is that a full enough picture, Briggs? Or shall I give more...."

Suddenly, without warning, Ram Singh reeled backward, his head knocked back between his shoulders. Briggs snatched his leather portfolio and sprang past Nita against the wall.

"If one of you moves," he cried sharply, "the ship sinks!" He held the portfolio raised above his head, a gun in the other hand.

"Nonsense, Briggs," Kirkpatrick growled. "That bag couldn't possibly hold enough gas to sink this ship."

Briggs laughed shrilly. "It holds enough to release the big tank of gas I have hidden aboard the ship. The ventilation system of the ship will carry this to it. Your guns are useless. I released gas into the room when I first entered, just a little, but enough to make your guns explode if you fire them. My own weapon is impervious to the gas."

Anse Collins was crouched with his fists clenched, his eyes glaring. Nancy Collins had shrunk back from Briggs and Nita picked herself up slowly from the floor where Briggs had hurled her. She dropped the wig from her hands with a shudder of distaste.

"Give up, Briggs," Kirkpatrick snarled at him. "You can't escape…."

Briggs' gun came up slowly. "Oh, yes, I can," he said. "I can kill you all—my southern accent again—take your plane and release the gas. Yes, I think I should escape."

"The Spider has your daughter captive," Wentworth said quietly.

BRIGGS GLARED at him. "I shall make you tell where she is, Wentworth," he said curtly. "Talk, or your Nita shall suffer terribly before she dies. A bullet through her white belly… There's no use in pretending you're not the Spider. I know you are. This stuff about getting that story from Bee Ross… That's all hokum!"

"My gun also is impervious to the gas," Wentworth put in quietly. His weapon was leveled at the little man's stomach.

"A bluff," snarled Briggs, "a bluff that will get you nowhere!"

Abruptly he sprang sideways, flung his arms about Nita van Sloan so that he held the pistol in front of her—the pistol and the portfolio.

"Grab his bag!" Wentworth snapped.

Nita snaked her arms from out of his grip, seized the portfolio with both hands. Briggs snarled, raked at her head with his automatic and she reeled forward, but she still clutched at the bag, doubled her body forward to protect it. Wentworth sprang sideways, his automatic jerking up, but Briggs was too swift for him. The small man bounded like a rubber ball, went out through the suite's door into the hall and banged the barrier shut behind him. He blasted lead through the panel and Collins dropped to the floor, his left leg shattered by a bullet. He cursed violently. Nancy, flung down on her knees beside him, shielding him with her body from more lead.

"Oh, Anse," she moaned. "God, don't let him die!"

Briggs shouted outside the door.

"The first man to open the door dies," Briggs bellowed. "Remember your guns are useless."

Wentworth charged the door and wrenched it open, hurling himself aside. More lead streamed through the opening, hammering the wall. Kirkpatrick, who had rushed forward, stopped with a grunt, sat down heavily with both arms locked across his belly. He staggered to his feet and pulled a shattered gun from his belt. Briggs' bullet had struck there. He reeled a moment, sank weakly down to the floor. He wasn't injured badly but the blow had paralyzed his muscles.

"Master," Ram Singh's voice was sharp but low at Wentworth's elbow. "I could climb out through the porthole."

"Say it loudly," Wentworth whispered, and the Hindu repeated, as if he were calling from across the room.

"Master, if I could get past the door, I could climb out the porthole."

"I'll knock out the light," Wentworth called back. He did that, then thrust his gun into his belt, sprang for the door and caught the lintel with both hands. He swung with his feet doubled up and landed softly on all fours in the hallway. No shot welcomed him and his lips skinned back from his teeth in a tight, fierce grin. His ruse had worked, had drawn Briggs away from his guard in fear that he might be flanked.

DARTING SOFT-FOOTED along the hall, Wentworth swiftly figured out the geography of the ship, where the ventilation system would shoot the fumes that Briggs had planned to release in the stateroom. He frowned as he ran, shook his head. It was nonsense. The ventilators did not blow out of the rooms. They blew fresh air into them. He should have grasped that at once. The whole thing had been a bluff. Briggs had come into the suite without any suspicion that he might be exposed and had cleverly seized on a ruse to stall off capture.

A picture flashed into Wentworth's mind. Eddie Blanton telling of the destruction of the pirate yacht. "A tank on the deck," he had said. Wentworth recalled abruptly that he had seen a cylindrical tank in the forward deck-well, lashed to the deck. He threw caution to the winds and sprinted.

Wentworth plunged into the opening from which the man had issued, found a narrow companionway winding upward. He grabbed the rails and yanked himself up the steps, reached the deck above and spun out into the open.

Wentworth streaked forward along the deck, sprang to the railing. The well was in shadow, but he made out the cylindrical form of the tank, made out a man hunched above it.

"Get away from that tank, Briggs," he roared, "or by heaven I'll shoot the heart out of you."

Mocking laughter floated up to him and the cover clanged against metal as Briggs wrenched it from the tank. Good God! What was Briggs yelling?

"Too late, Spider," he jeered from the darkness. "You're too late. You can't reach me in time to stop the gas. You can't shoot because your gun will blow up...."

Wentworth sent his wild laughter into the night. "I can shoot, Briggs!" he shouted. "I had a gun plated with gold for just this emergency..." He plucked an oiled rag that protected the inside of the barrel from the muzzle, threw a half dozen shots at that huddled figure on top the tank.

He sprang to the rail, balanced for an instant, then sprang out into the darkness toward the steel deck of the well.

Briggs' scream came again, nearly inarticulate words. "You... damned..." It mingled pain and startled surprise, then changed to a piercing shriek of absolute terror.

Wentworth's feet banged on the deck and he sprawled on hands and knees, his gun flying from his hand. He fought to his feet, lunged toward the bulk of the tank. He could no longer see Briggs, but in his nostrils was an acrid burning odor. It strangled him, bit at his eyes. He knew what that was. The steel-eater had escaped, but had enough of it got out to soften the *Britannia's* plates?

WITH A sob, he flung himself on the tank, groping with nails that grated painfully on its sides for the lid that Briggs had removed. He heard the Master screaming, heard him beg for mercy, and the sounds were hollow. They were accompanied by a muffled clangor of leather beating steel.

As Wentworth's groping hands found the lid, he realized what had happened. His bullets sprayed into the darkness had struck Briggs and bowled him into the opening of the tank of gas! Remembering what had happened to that other man who had been caught in a concentrated fog of the steel-eater, Wentworth felt a horror stab into his soul. Briggs was being eaten alive by the gas!

But there could be no hesitancy. Moments were precious. Already enough of the gas might have escaped to sink the *Britannia*. If he paused to haul Briggs from his torture chamber, more of the vicious steel eater would leak out. The ship would certainly be doomed. Wentworth's shoulders swelled. He seized the round metal lid of the tank's manhole and with a heave slapped it into place. Its clang was hollow and cracked and Brigg's rising scream was muted.

"Soap!" Wentworth yelled at the bridge. "Get soap and swab down the decks and plates! Fast, man!"

Behind him, he heard Kirkpatrick catch up the cry. The Commissioner had recovered from that bullet blow against his stomach, realized what he was doing, realized that soap would counteract the acid effect of the steel-eater.

The ship was safe and Wentworth's head wrenched back between his shoulders as the fearful grim laughter bubbled from his lips. He was laughing with fierce pleasure, the laughter that comes from the gods when a human monster's own works turn upon him and destroys him. And he was echoing, too, the shout of triumph with which the world hails cosmic retribution. Thinking of the tens of thousands that had died, the tens of thousands more that would go through life as cripples because this man had longed for gold, Wentworth reached for the turn-buckles that would secure the lid of the tank and seal Briggs in his cell of acid gas—gas that concentrated as it was here, would eat through living, human flesh.

And as Brigg's muffled screams of agony, his beating upon the walls that imprisoned him grew weaker, Wentworth leaned against the tank and his hands shook. Finally the sounds ceased within and the Spider lifted a drawn face toward the stars that shed dim light down upon the *Britannia*, upon the two thousand souls he had saved. And the Spider shuddered.

"It was horrible," he said hoarsely. "But it was necessary and it was just God knows it was just!"